Whiting Village School

dear
author

dear
author

*students write
about
the books that
changed
their lives*

Collected by
Weekly Reader's *Read* Magazine

Introduction by
Lois Lowry

CONARI PRESS
Berkeley, California

Conari Press books are distributed by Publishers Group West

ISBN: 1-57324-003-6

Cover design by Kathy Warriner

Library of Congress Cataloging-in-Publication Data
Dear author : students write about the books that changed their lives / collected by weekly reader's Read magazine ; introduction by Lois Lowry.
    p.   cm.
    Includes bibliographical references and index.
    Summary: A collection of letters from students to an assortment of authors both past and present about the impact of their work on the lives of their readers.
    ISBN 1-57324-003-6 (trade paper)
  1. Students—United States—Books and reading.   2. Authors and readers—United States— Correspondence.   3. Children's literature—Appreciation—United States.   4. Students— United States—Correspondence. [1. Authors—Correspondence.   2. Students—Correspon- dence.   3. Letters.   4. Books and reading.]   I. Read magazine.

  Z1037.A1D3   1995
  028.5'5—dc20   95-14455

Printed in the United States of America on recycled paper
10 9 8 7 6 5 4 3 2

contents

the letters

about this book

"Books are more than paper with little black marks. They can be complete worlds. While I was reading your book Where the Red Fern Grows, *I had two places to live. Even though I might be in my bedroom or in the car while reading, I was with Billy, right next to him as he went through all his ups and downs in his adventures."*

—from a letter to Wilson Rawls by Kristin Knutson, 12
Elmbrook Middle School, Brookfield, Wisconsin

Dear Reader,

Get ready.

The book you are about to read is a window to other worlds—the personal lives of young people today. It is not easy to write honestly about painful memories or even happy ones. It is not easy to admit your weaknesses or needs or dreams. But this is just what the young authors in this collection have done.

The book came about in this way. *Read* is a literary magazine for middle and senior high-school students, published by the Weekly Reader Corporation. For thirteen years, *Read* and The Center for the Book at the Library of Congress have cosponsored a national essay contest called Letters About

Literature. Each fall, *Read's* editors invite students in grades six through twelve to write a personal letter to the author of a book that has in some way changed the students' way of thinking. "Forget the dry-as-dust plot summaries," we challenge our students. "Forget analyzing themes. After all, you are writing to the author, and he or she already knows what the book is about. What the author doesn't know is how the book affected *you*. Write about you," we encourage them. "Make a link between yourself and a character or an event in the story."

Each December, the letters stream into our editorial offices. Over the past two years, nearly twenty thousand young adults have entered our contest. These young writers did not disappoint us. Their letters were personal, conversational, amusing, and, in some instances, upsetting. They wrote about their triumphs and failures to authors both living and dead. Each letter is different because each student-author is different. But the one thing the letters have in common is this: None of the letters is indifferent.

Now we are sharing a selection of those very personal letters with you. If you want to know what young people are reading, get ready. If you want to know what young people are thinking about the world in which they live, get ready. There is some very good writing here and a lot of good reading. Kristin Knutson is right. Books are worlds. And these letters are the windows to those worlds.

Catherine Gourley
Editor, *Read* magazine

introduction

When I was young, I thought that all writers were creatures with mythical status: unavailable, inaccessible, perhaps dead. It never occurred to me to conceive of them as real human beings, in a house somewhere, drinking coffee, using a dictionary, making typing errors, chewing on a pencil eraser, twisting a strand of hair (or stroking a beard) as they thought of the next sentence.

Imaginative though I was as a kid, I never pictured a mailman knocking at the door of a writer and saying something mundane like, "Lots of mail from your fans today." Nor could I envision the writer opening a letter, reading a letter, or chuckling or weeping at a letter from a person like me.

Yet here I sit today, chewing on a strand of hair while I ponder a sentence, and on my desk is a stack of mail from readers who realize that I am no farther away from them than a first-class stamp.

I wish I were young again, with a favorite book by my side and a pen and paper in my hand.

Dear Lois Lenski, I just read a book that you wrote. It is called Indian Captive. *The girl in it, Mary, had hair the same light color as mine, and so the Indians called her "Corn-Tassel." Now I sometimes think of myself as "Corn-*

Tassel" and I try to be as brave as she was. I don't tell anybody about that because they would laugh. But I think you would understand.

That's a letter I would have written when I was nine.

At ten, I would have written to a woman named Betty Smith, to thank her for creating a little girl named Francie Nolan in a book called *A Tree Grows in Brooklyn*. She was my best friend when we were both in sixth grade, though her life in the boisterous immigrant neighborhoods of Brooklyn seemed infinitely more exciting and dangerous than mine in a Pennsylvania college town. I envied Francie her raucous surroundings, shared her most private fears and worries, and have remembered her with love for almost fifty years.

When I was eleven, I met a boy named Jody Baxter and learned all there was to know about grief.

Dear Marjorie Kinnan Rawlings, I have never lived in the South, I have never been poor, I have never been a boy. But when I read The Yearling, *I understood Jody, and I understood how he felt when his pet fawn had to be killed because it ate the crops. I had to give my dog Punky away because he bit my little brother. I know Punky didn't mean to. Now my heart is broken. You and Jody know how that feels.*

Dear Gustave Flaubert, I would have written, when I was fifteen and felt that my life was as dull and unrewarding as Emma Bovary's. At sixteen, making the acquaintance of Holden Caulfield, it would have been an ongoing, slightly sardonic thank-you note to Salinger—at least until I turned seventeen and began to compose, in my mind, a more impassioned and convoluted correspondence with Thomas Hardy.

Somehow the communications I actually *did* put on paper—usually in garish turquoise ink (which seemed terribly soigné)— never amounted to more than perfunctory thank-you notes to great-aunts and grandparents after Christmas. *The sweater fits perfectly and will look nice with my new gray skirt.* There had never been the underlying level of communication that would have enabled me to speak the truth, even if one could write truths in such appalling ink:

> *The sweater fits just fine but, oh, Aunt Grace, I wish I had a more grown-up body to put inside it, and I wonder whether I will ever be pretty, and whether boys will ever like me, and I know you will understand. . . .*

No. One can't write such things to a person who will be sitting across the dinner table from you on Sunday, suggesting another helping of peas.

Privacy is required. Distance. And a different kind of gift for which to say thank you. Look at what these young letter-writers have to say, about their favorite books, to the authors:

> . . . it has left a spot in my heart . . .
> It comforted me a lot . . .
> It opened me to what I am . . .
> Your book has helped me find my place . . .

I needed someone to remind me that I can really make my *life work* . . .

Some of the authors to whom these letters are addressed are, in fact, dead. They are not drinking coffee, chewing a pencil stub, or stroking their beards—not in this world, at least. Yet how alive they are—Anne Frank, Malcolm X, John Steinbeck, and the others—how accessible, how available, to each young reader.

What a gift they bring, author and reader, to each other.

Here's another unwritten letter from me to someone who changed my life:

Dear Harper Lee, Thank you for writing To Kill a Mockingbird. *I became Scout when I read the book and I have been Scout ever since. She (and you) taught me about innocence and honor. Thank you for never writing another book about her and her brother.*

I have grandchildren now. I can watch with delight as they turn pages that invite them into the lives of Scout, Jody, Francie, Corn-Tassel, Holden Caulfield, and others I have never met. But I can't participate in those friendships between writer and reader. Those are private.

The phrase *Dear Author* is not just a simple formal salutation. It's a whisper that touches on a love affair. We should listen to it with envy and with awe.

Lois Lowry

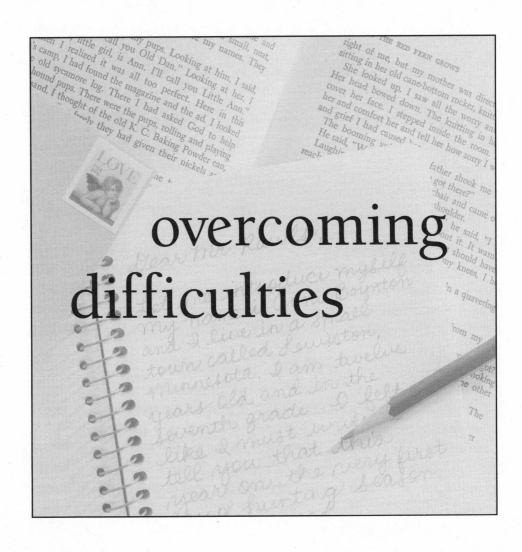

overcoming difficulties

> **Carl Lewis** is one of the premier athletes of our time. He dominated track and field throughout the 1980s, winning four Olympic gold medals in 1984 and two in 1988. In addition, he broke the world record in 1991 for the hundred-meter dash.

Mr. Carl Lewis,

Well, I'm in school now and back on track. Last year I dropped out. Thanks to your book, *Inside Track*, I was given the inspiration to, as you put it, "look forward." Initially, I selected your book because we have common interests in sports and running. After reading the first two chapters, I realized we shared much more.

I am a shy runt, too, just like you said you were. You might have been the smallest in your family, but last year I was the smallest in my whole school—4'6". Most kids considered me the school nerd. Kids pushed me around the halls, stole my glasses, and in general made life miserable. As you know, prejudice comes in all forms. A lot happened and I could not handle it. I ached with that hollow emptiness you expressed with the loss of your father. April 1, my grandfather died. I left school in the spring of last year, drifting without direction.

Sports has always been my life. It was the only thread I had to hang on to. I don't have a team or a coach, only my little brother, Michael. He is two and a half years younger than me. People always ask if we are twins. We play in the same way you did by setting up track meets in our yard. I had to laugh about how you handed out your mom's medals at your meets. I bet she laughs now too even though she didn't then. Your mom sounds like a very special lady. You spoke with such love and affection about your parents. I feel the same about my family. Unlike you, my parents are not athletes, but they help us all they can.

A big race was coming up. It wasn't your Olympics, but for me it was just as important. The Arizona Iron Kids Triathlon race was the place I wanted to carry home a victory in memory of my grandfather. I think you could under-stand, since you expressed a desperate need to bring the gold home in your dad's honor after his death. Usually, we don't travel much to races. It is just too expensive. Mom and Dad knew what this one meant to me, so it was a go. Grandmother came for support. I was ready, but nervous. It was good to hear that even the pros like you get on edge before a race.

I got off to a great start and was out of the swimming pool well in front of my competition. I held the lead on the first bike loop. I knew I could outrun my field if I could get a respectable bike time. As I came into the bike marking zone, the official accidentally hooked me with his arm as he marked the inside of my elbow instead of the outside of my arm. All eighty pounds of me went flying over the front of my handlebars, along with my dreams of a win for Grandfather. My right side slammed into the pavement. Blood streamed from my shoulder to my ankle. Ambulance drivers tried to assist me, but I shoved them away and got back on my bike. The sportsmanship award I received wasn't the gold I had worked so hard for. Like you, I just wanted to run the race I had trained for. The official dashed my dreams like Ben Johnson had shattered yours. By June, I reached an all-time low when I discovered your book.

It was like a light bulb flashed on. You explained so many things that were brewing inside me about life and sports. I wasn't alone anymore. You were there with me. Your book taught me that size and circumstances don't matter as much as goals and persistence. You said you had a turning point in your sophomore year when you messed up for your teammates. If Carl Lewis could mess up and turn it around, I began to think I could, too. As I turned the pages, I experienced someone who really understood how I felt. You became a friend to me because you understood how I felt. People think you just go out and run. The clock is the only enemy you have. We know there is so much more to it. Drugs, politics, press, coaches, peers, and more—all affect the outcome of a race, and life.

Inside Track really turned things around for me. I started working even harder on my training and academics by setting realistic goals and striding ahead. Over the summer, my brother and I helped to earn enough to go to the Youth Triathlon National Championships in Nashville. It was our first national race. I thought a lot about what advice you would give me. Your book echoed, "Just run your race. Focus."

Mr. Lewis, I did just that. I wish I could tell you I won the triathlon over all senior girls, but I can't. I am proud to say, though, that I beat the winner's swim by eighteen seconds and outran her by seven seconds. My run was the fastest-ranked run of the senior girls in the United States at the national championships.

You helped me to turn it around and run in the right direction. I really needed to let you know that *Inside Track* is an inspiration and guiding light to me. The warm, honest sharing of your experiences has given me the courage to go beyond pain and frustration. Frankness regarding what you experienced encouraged me to risk whatever the future holds.

Katherine Niblett, 14
Laguna Middle School, San Luis Obispo, CA
Teacher: Mrs. Shimke

Popular author **Judy Blume**'s works include *Are You There, God? It's Me, Margaret; It's Not the End of the World; Tales of a Fourth Grade Nothing;* and *Otherwise Known as Sheila the Great.* Another letter about her books can be found in "Self-Discovery."

Dear Judy Blume,

Your book *It's Not the End of the World* sent me a more powerful message than I have ever received in my life. My parents had been separated for about a year and a half when I first read it, and I still had not accepted that I lived with only one of my parents, instead of both.

Many strong emotions swept over me as I finished the last chapter, the strongest being anger. I was angry with you for making me face the truth—that my parents wouldn't be getting back together. I was angry with myself for reading your book. But most of all, I was angry with my parents for becoming like Ellie and Bill.

Weeks later, when I had tamed my anger, disappointment crashed down on me. I was disappointed because of the ending—Ellie and Bill would not be reunited. In books, there is always a fairy-tale ending. Two people fight, they yell, but in the end they realize that they still love each other and they live happily ever after. Only, it wasn't like that in your book, and, unfortunately, it wasn't like that in my life.

It wasn't fair, I decided. It wasn't fair that Karen's and my parents were not together. All of my friends' parents were together, so why was I different? I wasn't going to let on that I cared. That was the final decision I made. If I kept everything bottled up, maybe the problem would disappear.

I kept things hidden for so long, though, that my mom took us to a family counselor. "Us" was she, my brother, and me. I was convinced that I was fine, that I didn't need to go. But after eight sessions, I learned to deal with the brutal truth. Only the truth didn't seem so brutal anymore, and I didn't feel so alone.

Now, I have a new stepfather and a new brother. I see my father every day when he picks up my brother and me from school. My mother is home after school, and they get along. My father and my stepfather get along as well. That's not to say that everything is always great. Sometimes one of us is in a bad mood or someone is overtired. Usually, though, our household runs pretty smoothly.

It was a rough five years, and while things have started to fall in place, some things will never be the same. I will never again wake up at 4 A.M. and find my dad in the bathroom, shaving. I will never kiss him before I go to bed each night. He will never have another chance to walk into my bedroom at night and pull down my blinds and turn off my light. All these things are a part of my childhood, which isn't yet over.

It's Not the End of the World taught me to face my challenges, to share my feelings, and, most of all, to have an open mind. Tomorrow I'll be a different person than I am today, and next week I'll be different than I will be tomorrow. Throughout my ordeal, my hopes, my dreams, my *life* have changed dramatically. But one thing will always be the same, no matter how old I get. I will still have my memories of helping Dad shave at dawn and of kissing him each night. I will have memories of climbing into Dad and Mom's bed.

And do you know something? It's okay that they're just memories. Now I can accept that.

Annie-Laurie Breen, 12
St. Gabriel School, San Francisco, CA
Teacher: Ms. Lynn Grier

John Gunther was born in Chicago, Illinois, in 1901 and worked as a foreign correspondent, author, network radio commentator, and lecturer. Although his most famous book is *Death Be Not Proud*, his writings include the Inside series *(Inside Asia, Inside Africa,* and *Inside USA), The Golden Fleece,* and *Roosevelt in Retrospective: A Profile in History.* The following two letters offer very different reactions to Gunther's work.

Dear Mr. Gunther,

"The doctors will come out, shaking their heads in disbelief, saying, 'She's one in a million.'" That's what the psychic said, and normally I don't believe in that, but this time she was right.

The person who's one in a million is my grandmother, and last year she was diagnosed with pancreatic cancer, a deadly disease where only 15 percent of people diagnosed live. But my grandmother had a successful operation and came home to stay—or so we thought. At her six-month checkup, she was told that her cancer had metastasized to her liver—and the doctors said there was nothing they could do.

I just happened to pick up your book and, as I read, I realized that *Death Be Not Proud* had subconsciously impacted my life.

Your sad yet triumphant saga of your son Johnny taught me what I, as just a small part of a large family, could do. Johnny seems mirrored through the actions of my grandmother. She never complains, never "burdens" us with her constant aches, always puts us first, and she, like Johnny, asks 'Why?' But I'm afraid no one can answer that question. I'm afraid none of us really know how she feels. I'm afraid that there really is no hope. And I'm afraid my grandmother will die.

Thanks to your book and through reading about the struggles that Johnny endured, I realize that I *can* help. I *can* be there and be strong for her, and I *can* have love for her.

But none of us—although we try—can remove the fear.

Rebecca Godsil, 14
Galesburg High School, Galesburg, IL
Teacher: Miss S. L. Hinman

Dear John Gunther,

I write this letter not on a desk trimmed in gold, not on paper signed by a foreign king, nor do I write this now with a pen given to me as a gift from a great poet. I write this now only with the knowledge of a gift of more value and love than any other imaginable: the gift of my hands, the body it's connected to, the soul it captures, and the mind it encapsulates. I learned of this wonderful gift from reading your book *[Death Be Not Proud]*.

I read it because I hoped it would give me a better understanding of why my grandparents, two of the most important people in my life, had to die. I slowly realized that to dwell on their deaths would be wrong. Instead I came to know that I should truly spend my time thanking them for the two most important people of my life, my mother and father.

My parents were never the friends I sometimes wish they were, but your book gave me something else to think about. It showed me a perspective I would otherwise never have seen.

I began your book after a huge argument with my father over a very small matter. I really thought that my father hated me at that moment. As I read, you expressed such pride in your son, it made me wonder how my father would describe me. Trying to remember how my father had once described me, I could not find one of the words *hate* or even *dislike*. My memory did give me a picture of a proud father, rattling off to a complete stranger everything that made his child so "gifted."

Death Be Not Proud gave me, a growing child, one of the most valuable lessons to be learned: that my parents love me now and will always.

Sabrina Cambone, 14
Peru Central School, Peru, NY
Teacher: Mrs. Donna Kemp

> **Go Ask Alice** is based on the actual diary of a fifteen-year-old drug user.

Dear Anonymous Author,

I have recently read your book *Go Ask Alice*. I have to tell you that reading this book made me cry, laugh, and sometimes want to kill myself. Reading your book was like reading my own life, word for word, page for page.

During the period of reading the book, I had a serious drug problem. I did the same things as Alice. I can remember feeling so much pain for the girl in the book and then turning around and thinking, *If you're crying over the girl in the story, you might as well be crying for yourself!* I was pretty messed up. I never ran away from home, but I did stay away a lot. And I ended up in a lot of the same situations. Being at what seemed like a real normal party with a lot of respectable people, and then BAMM!! Something is dropped in your drink and the next thing you know you're sitting in a corner isolated from all reality and tripping out pretty bad. Then the next day, you have found your drug for the next month until something stronger comes along.

It took me a long time to finish the story, but as I read it, I started realizing that drugs are no good for me. They're just going to get me into a lot of trouble, not that they hadn't already. As the story went on, sometimes I felt it would be neat to just pack up and go somewhere away from my family and everything. To leave just like Alice and start my own life, living by myself. I was almost to the point where I was gonna go. My parents were on my back, I had lost most of my friends, and felt as if everyone was trying to get something from me, instead of thinking that they were trying to help me! I was just another street druggy who didn't know reality from fiction.

I didn't leave after all. Something held me back. The more I read the book and saw that it didn't work out for Alice, I was glad I didn't leave either. I would have been really scared and more lonely than I was before.

I started to keep a diary like Alice, but my reasons were different. I wanted to keep one because I thought it would somehow get me off drugs. I thought that I would keep a journal of how I felt on the drug, which was crystal most of the time, and then how I felt when I was coming down. I would write for about a month and then reread it. I was sure that when I reread it that it would make me so sick that I would quit! But it never happened. Yeah, I would read it, and it would make me cry and feel real sorry for myself, and then the next day I would tell my boyfriend, "That's it, I'm through." He would hug me and understand. But then later that day, there I'd be in the girl's bathroom sniffing white stuff off a glass mirror and praying to GOD that no one would come in the bathroom! And no one ever did. So then I'd forget about the promise I made to myself, and I'd start the routine all over. I told myself I was gonna quit at least once a week. But it never happened. I was hooked. Drugs were my life. I knew that after awhile. Kinda like Alice. She always told herself that she was gonna quit. But just like me, it never happened. Except I got out before she did.

I can remember sniffing in my third-period class on top of the desk while watching a movie. That was so crazy! If I were to get caught it would have been over for me! But when you're a tweaker, you don't care.

I can't believe all this crashed down on my head only six months ago, when I finally came clean and told my parents. Man was my mom [furious]! I knew I had hurt her so bad by doing this. I can remember her telling me how stupid she felt cause she didn't know. For over a year, I had fooled her. It wasn't that—I just covered up really well. I got real skinny! I got down to about a hundred pounds, maybe less. My skin color was pasty white; I was brittle and felt rundown all the time. My parents started to get a little suspicious when I accidentally wore shorts around them. I was always real concerned about my weight and I was always complaining. So they thought I was on diet pills.

People look down on me for what I did in the past. It doesn't bother me though. I feel it wasn't their life, so they shouldn't care. I sometimes get the urge to tweak again. I catch myself saying, "One time won't hurt me," exactly what I said the first time I ever did it, along with "I won't ever do it again!" I have been clean from tweak for six months. I'm very proud of myself. I have made it through the toughest part of my life. I did it. I got through and I'm still alive! I will survive! No matter that it takes, I will SURVIVE!

The end of your book was very upsetting. I cried when I read that the person you wrote about had died of a drug overdose. But I'm not gonna give up like that; I'm gonna live my life and maybe write a story like you did only about myself. I feel sorry for you. But I thank you 'cause, believe it or not, you helped me a lot to get through some tough times in my life. Or maybe I just thought you did 'cause I had no one else to help me!

I'm slowly taking the road that I have always wanted to be on. And escaping from the one that almost ruined my life. There is so much out there for me. I can be and do anything that I want. I just hope that I follow my dreams and someday leave my past in the gutter!

Kim Lawrence, 17
Chula Vista School, Chula Vista, CA
Teacher: Ms. Susan Denis

Steven Levenkron is one of America's foremost therapists in the area of obsessive-compulsive disorders. His other works include *Kessa, Treating and Overcoming Anorexia Nervosa*, and *Obsessive-Compulsive Disorders*.

Dear Steven Levenkron,

It was quite clear to me that something was terribly wrong. Mary, my best friend, was not herself, nor had she been for a long time. At first, my friends and I overlooked the problem. But as time raced forward, so did the frequent, prolonged visits to the hospital. MARY WAS NOT EATING. She seemed to grow paler and thinner each day. Her flesh was no longer a rosy peach, but purple and cold. Her gaunt figure and depressed demeanor haunted me. She was distant, withdrawn. The illness that had so evilly invaded her became apparent—anorexia nervosa. No description can adequately portray the pain my friend was going through. But Mary did not share her anguish nor anything she was going through.

Grief, confusion, fear—emotions swelled inside me. I had no escape and nowhere to turn. No one could comfort me or answer my pleas. Then I discovered *The Best Little Girl in the World*. Kessa transported me to her world. She diminished the chaos taking place in my mind. I began to understand anorexia— maybe not so much as why it had infected Mary, but I began to comprehend her situation.

It has been two years since reading your book, one year since Mary's death. I struggled to shut out anorexia and Mary completely. The pain was too much to bear. I plunged deep into depression. Luckily, I was able to turn myself around. I realize now that memories of Mary, some painful, will never go away. It has been hard for me to become close to anyone again. I have decided to pick up your book and make the journey once again into Kessa's world. Maybe now I can complete the path of full recovery.

Alicia Ogram, 13
The Newport School, Kensington, MD
Teacher: Mrs. Marcus

From the age of one and a half, **Helen Keller** could not hear, see, or speak. She lived in a dark and isolated world until Anne Sullivan came to teach her. As an adult, Helen Keller traveled all over the world and raised money to start schools for deaf and blind children. Her courage and determination earned her admiration and respect as she set out to help others conquer the odds against them.

Dear Helen Keller,

Your book, *The Story of My Life*, has changed my whole outlook on life. I now feel that anyone can accomplish just about any goal they choose to. You have shown the whole world that being disabled does not mean you are stupid or untalented. Your story gives hope to many. I used to think that disabled people just could not do very many things.

I am totally deaf in my left ear. I do not know if I was born this way, or if my loss was caused by an infection or a high fever. My parents did not realize I had a problem until I was about two and a half years old. I have a twin sister, and her hearing is fine.

Before my parents realized that I had a problem, they thought I just did not listen to them. When someone spoke on my left side, I simply did not hear everything. I was very frustrated, as were my parents. Sometimes I threw tantrums. People began to think I was a brat. Finally, my hearing loss was discovered, and as long as everyone talked to me on my right side, and made sure I heard them, I listened to what I was told. My parents decided that I was not such a brat after all.

When I started school, I wore a hearing aid that crossed the sound over to my good ear. It helped some, but it was also a pain. Kids were always making fun of me, always asking questions. My hearing aids made me different. They always fell out if I tried to play on the playground equipment also. I felt sorry for myself.

At age eleven, I decided I was not going to wear them anymore. I learned to make do with one ear. I always turn my head toward my good ear when someone is talking to me. I manage fine.

Until I read your book, I think I felt a little sorry for myself. I resented not having normal hearing like my sister and brother. Now, I know just how lucky I am. You accomplished so much with your disabilities, it almost made me ashamed for feeling so sorry for myself. There are so many people with problems worse than mine. Your story gives hope to people with any type of disability. I will never forget this book and how much courage you had.

Michelle Elwood, 14
Eagle Point High School, Eagle Point, OR
Teacher: Mrs. Elaine Ledbetter

Dear Ms. Julie Reece Deaver,

I would like to thank you for your book, *Say Goodnight, Gracie.* I first read it a couple of years ago and (young as I was) I found it depressing and missing the air of romance that I at that time craved. It seems ironic to look back on my attitude then, because now I can realize that it is, in fact, a love story. Not because it was romantic or exotic at all, but because it tells about love and loss in a way I didn't understand then.

Love was a word that I thought I knew all about and that I looked upon in reverence. At the time, I was overlooking the only sort of love I knew; that I did not know the extent of. It was May of that year that I had a theater performance. Distinctly, I remember falling asleep that night, exhausted and ecstatic.

The next morning my parents woke me up and told me my brother was dead. Grief and pain have blocked out most of May and June. I can no longer remember them. Now, so much later, I have to strain to remember exactly how my brother was before the accident. Only small things remain clear. His smile. His eyes.

As time went on, other things invaded my life, and I began to feel the need to pull my family back together. My parents would cry openly. I remember my mother on her knees before my grandmother, rocking and screaming, "Mommy! Mommy! My baby's dead! My baby's dead!" My poor, frightened younger brother and sisters would cry in confusion and frustration. They could barely understand what was happening and I was too stunned and angry to help them.

Until my brother died, there were many things I did not understand. The most important is that I loved my brother. The most painful is that I never got a chance to tell him so. I would give anything in the world to tell him how much I loved him and needed him and how much I miss him.

Two weeks ago, I found your book in the library of my grief counseling center. I checked it out and spent the entire night reading it and crying. I more than understood the feelings Morgan had after Jimmy's death; I recognized them as my own. When my brother died I became very depressed—even at times suicidal. Your book had something that I missed the first time I read it: a message of hope. By the end, Morgan knew that however terrible Jimmy's death was, Morgan would live through it. You were right; there are people in our lives we don't think we will ever live without. I have learned our very strength is that we can.

Natalie Prado, 15
East Lansing High School, East Lansing, MI
Teacher: Mrs. Cassidy

Dear E. B. White,

I recently read your book *Charlotte's Web*. I enjoyed it very much and I want to tell you how it changed my life.

When I was in second or third grade, my parents got a divorce. My mother and I cried about it and talked about it, just like Fern took care of Wilbur in the beginning and helped him grow up to take care of himself. But, unfortunately, I fell into a deep depression. I felt just like Wilbur felt in your book. I was not special, useful, or worth anything. Anytime a person called me a name, I cried, making me feel more worse than before. Thank goodness I had a friend to help—my mom. When I felt down or in emotional stress, my mom was there to help. Just like Charlotte drew new webs to make Wilbur feel special and to save his life, my mom helped me feel special.

Another blow came in January 1993 when my Grandpa died of Alzheimer's disease. I again went into a deep depression. This time it was much more serious. Every time I was reminded of Grandpa, I cried. I missed my Grandpa very much and wanted to have him back, but that never could be. My mom helped me understand my problems and kept my spirits up like Charlotte helped keep Wilbur's spirits up.

I am in ninth grade now and have a new perspective on life. I just keep on living and trying, partially from the inspiration of your book. I now have more friends, enjoy life much more, and get better grades because my perspective on life has changed for the better. My life has been more enriched, is more exciting, and I have more opportunities to do things that I never would have had if I had not been inspired by the character of Wilbur.

I would really like to thank you for creating the characters of Wilbur, Charlotte, and Fern in your book, *Charlotte's Web.*

Chris Bailey, 14
Carthage Junior High School, Carthage, MO
Teacher: Mrs. Claudia Mundell

Robyn Miller, who suffered from cystic fibrosis, lived in a world of oxygen masks, medications and special diets. After her death, her parents authorized the publication of *Robyn's Book: A True Diary*.

Dear Parents of Robyn,

I'm sorry about the loss of your daughter. She was very strong and she loved her family very much. I too have Cystic Fibrosis (C.F.), but I'm only thirteen. When I started reading her book, I thought, is that what's going to happen to me? I have a great life right now. I go to the doctor for a checkup every six months. I have great lungs, but so did Robyn. I guess I'm writing you this note because if I go into the hospital, I want to have the courage and strength to fight this disease. Robyn was not scared to die, and I want not to be scared. I learned a lot from Robyn. I really didn't know much about C.F., and my parents didn't like to talk about it much. I really would have liked to meet her and ask how she gets up every morning, knowing she has a hard day in front of her. Once in a while, I'm so scared I don't want to go to the hospital, but I have to so I can make sure I'm doing fine.

Last year, I was at the doctor's and they found something in my lungs. They gave me some medicine to try to make that stuff go away. I worked as hard as I could to get it gone. In those two weeks, I thought about how I took life and friends for granted. I used to think I would live until I was eighty or so, but I know the real truth—I'm not. All my friends know I have C.F. and they do not care. They like me for who I am. When I am down, they always cheer me up. They're really great. My parents worry about me a lot. I tell them I don't sit around and worry because then it would take over, and I won't let it ruin my life. I've heard about a lot of kids dying because of C.F., but I'm going to fight even if it takes my whole life.

Brandi Hayes, 13
St. Aloysius School, Springfield, IL
Teacher: Mrs. Roberta Hull

Erma Bombeck is a writer and columnist, whose work appears internationally in more than eight hundred newspapers. She is the author of many bestsellers, including *A Marriage Made in Heaven . . . or Too Tired for an Affair*, and *Family: The Ties That Bind . . . and Gag.* She was moved to write *I Want to Grow Up, I Want to Grow Hair, I Want to Go to Boise* when she visited a camp for children fighting cancer. Mrs. Bombeck lives in Arizona.

Dear Ms. Bombeck,

I Want to Grow Up, I Want to Grow Hair, I Want to Go to Boise is a wonderful book. The hope and optimism shown by the kids is so uplifting.

I was diagnosed with Ewing's Sarcoma of the spine when I was only sixteen years old, a sophomore in high school. Cancer changes everyone that is touched by it. The victim, the patients, the siblings, and friends are all affected by this disease.

I could really relate to the kids in the book. I never felt anger for the interruption of my teen years. I have never feared my future; I know I have hope. I never wanted pity—it was for the weak, and I had to be strong. Just as the kids in your book, I very quickly came to terms with my enemy and prepared for the battle of my life.

I knew I would have a future. I was prom queen and will graduate this spring at the top of my class. Cancer was simply an obstacle that I overcame. The road was long and treacherous, but I did make it to my final destination, a destination full of hope, health, and happiness.

Thank you for your heartwarming book. Finally, someone recognizes children who battle cancer every day of our lives. Thank you for showing the world that childhood cancer can be humorous. Humor is the best defense for cancer victims.

Kristy Hooker, 18
Breathitt County High School, Jackson, KY
Teacher: Lavonne Hubbard

Jean Davis Okimoto is a volunteer writing tutor in the Seattle Author Mentor Program and creator of the Mayor's Reading Awards for reading improvement in the Seattle public schools. Her published works include *Jason's Women; My Mother Is Not Married to My Father, It's Just Too Much;* and *Boomerang Kids: How to Live with Adult Children Who Return Home.* Ms. Okimoto has four grown children and lives in Seattle with her husband, Joe, and their dogs, Harold and Maude.

Dear Jean Okimoto,

I read *Molly By Any Other Name* and understand where you are coming from. I am adopted too. When I read your book, Molly seemed to become the friend I never had. She understood. I am only twelve years old, and when I become mad at my parents, I sometimes wonder who my birth mother was. I wonder if she would handle the situation the same way my parents do.

I know that if I ever find her, she can't be my mother. A mother is someone who takes care of you in the ups and the downs. Being a birth mother doesn't make you a real mother. She may be somebody else's mother, but never mine. I respect her for giving me up. I'll never despise her for that. She may have made a mistake, but that's human nature. If she didn't give me up, I could have become a burden for her and wouldn't be growing up in the environment I am today (a very good one, I may add). I respect her for giving me up. At least she didn't abort me.

I am grateful for my parents to take me. They wanted a child very much, and my birth mother gave them one. I love my parents very much and they love me. Thank you. Your book touched my life.

D'Lisa McKee, 13
Carthage Junior High School, Carthage, MO
Teacher: Claudia Mundell

Dear S. E. Hinton,

When I was eleven years old, I read your book *The Outsiders* for the first time. I will never forget everything that I learned from it. I began to really see that money does not determine how good a person is or what values he has. The Curtises hardly had any money, but their family learned to be rich with love. I appreciated this lesson that your book taught me, but it wasn't until I was fourteen years old that I understood the most important lesson of *The Outsiders.*

When I was fourteen, my friend Joy passed away. I suddenly could understand what Ponyboy was feeling when his best friend Johnny died. I was sad, confused, and angry. Most of all I didn't want to believe that she was really gone. Then one day I picked up my copy of *The Outsiders* and began to read it again. I realized that I was the same age that Ponyboy was—fourteen, too young to be thought of as an adult, too old to be carefree like a kid. As I continued to read, I began to notice so many things about Ponyboy that reminded me of myself: his sensitivity, loyalty, and struggle to be understood.

The next morning when I woke up, the sun was just beginning to rise. As I watched the sky brighten, I felt happy for the first time since Joy died. I thought about Ponyboy and how he always managed to see hope for the future, even after he had experienced a loss. That's when I knew just how precious life really is and that it shouldn't be taken for granted. Since then I've opened up my eyes to all of the little things that make life worth living—the sky, clouds, and sunrises and all the other things that I never really paid attention to before.

The Outsiders helped me through a difficult time in my life. It taught me that no matter what happens in life, there will always be hope for the future. I've read your book too many times to count, but I'll always remember the wonderful lessons that it taught me.

Sheri-Ann Sekiya, 15
Pearl City High School, Pearl City, HI
Teacher: Mrs. Miriam Rappolt

Wilson Rawls was born on a small farm in the Ozarks. He spent his youth prowling the river bottoms with his sole companion—a bluetick hound. His other works include *The Summer of the Monkeys*.

Dear Mr. Wilson Rawls,

Let me introduce myself. My name is Joni Boynton and I live in a small rural town called Lewiston, Minnesota. I am twelve years old and in the seventh grade. I felt like I must write to tell you that this year on the very first day of deer hunting season, I experienced some of the very same feelings of your main character, Billy, in your novel *Where the Red Fern Grows*.

It was just a week ago that I finished your novel. (By the way, I truly enjoyed it!) But it was not until my experience of just a few days ago that I realized how much my life had mirrored Billy's. You see, I had a dog named Bear that was shot by a very cruel hunter in three different areas of his rather small body.

This special dog of mine was always loyal and protective of not only our home but especially of myself. I could depend on him to walk me to the end of the driveway every single morning. He would be waiting my arrival shortly after five each evening. He would then proceed to lick and jump up on me to show his approval of my arriving home in time to play with him.

But today was different. Today my dog's life has ended and it has changed my life. As the day began, I heard a sound out in the yard, that of whines and cries of an injured animal in pain. Bear came to me in an almost lifeless walk. As I bent down to see him, I noticed he was covered with blood. He lay his head in my lap with such pain and agony it broke my heart. This episode seemed unreal. Why or how could anyone be so cruel? My dog is only knee-high and black in color. He was a Husky and by no imagination resembles a deer.

It is strange how an animal can become such an important part of your life. Knowing you have to care for it as you would a child, feeding it, keeping it clean, making sure it has all its shots and check-ups on a regular basis. And, of course, most importantly, loving it with your whole heart. This is by far the easiest of all the needs!

Loving just comes so easy and natural. Somehow, the love is returned a thousand times over. Someone like you would understand how this happens, because you have experienced it. The loss of an animal rips your heart apart, as if the gunshot had penetrated your own flesh!

The Red Fern continues to grow and make the burial. But for me, my dog's death will remind me of how autumn draws to a close and the red lights of Christmas will burn in my heart. Bear's blood-covered body will be significant of the season to begin.

Like Billy and his dogs, Dan and Ann, I will have to meet God halfway. I will have to put the memories of Bear away. To do that will take time. But each new day will help in the healing.

Mr. Rawls, I'm so glad that you wrote such a heartwarming novel. You see, it helps to know that someone else has gone through the same kind of pain. Maybe the sharing of the hurt is the halfway point. One shares a little bit of his life with another. It all boils down to sharing time. I spent time with my dog. I spent time reading your novel. One spends time on something of value.

Continue to write such great books—you will then continue to meet God halfway with helping someone else to heal!

Joni Boynton, 13
Lewiston-Altura High School, Lewiston, MN
Teacher: Ms. Lueck

Dear Beverly Cleary,

I have always thought that books had to make you laugh or cry, but the book I am going to write to you about, the one that inspired me, is the book entitled *Strider.*

Now there are many things that inspired me, but I will start off with the boy named Leigh. He is just like me. I am thirteen years old and Leigh is fourteen. He runs track, as do I. But the most important similarity is that my parents are divorced, too. My father never visits, and Leigh's dad rarely visits him; both dads always seem to be late on the support payments.

Another thing that affected me is the way you portrayed Leigh and his friend when they found the dog on the beach and they began to treat the dog like he was a child in a custody battle. They had to make up visitation rights on who would keep their dog at a certain house on a certain day, as well as who would get to walk him. All the other books I have read that are made for children of divorcing parents seem to have a little bit of fiction, but the book *Strider* seemed true to life without any made-up things. The most lasting feeling was that there are other people out there with the same exact problems, but, of course, some are not as severe.

Why did I choose the book? At first, I chose it because it was short and I could do my assignment with little work. However, as the story went on, I found myself very interested, to the point that I could not put the book down. It made me feel relieved to find out that I was normal and not that different than anyone else in this situation.

I would also like to know some things about you. Do you enjoy living in California? Have you ever been married and divorced? Are you also a child from a divorced family? I seem to feel you are, because of your insight into this very common but disturbing fact of life. I would like to hear from you, if possible.

Brandon Chrostowski, 14
Heritage Junior High School, Sterling Heights, MI
Teacher: Preston Staines

Howard Fast worked at several jobs, including as a page in the New York Public Library, before his first novel was published in 1932, when he was eighteen. He has been a writer in various forms since. His works include writings under the pseudonyms E. V. Cunningham and Walter Ericson. Some of his titles include *Spartacus* (adapted for the screen in 1960), *Strange Yesterday*, *The Picture-Book History of the Jews*, *Alice*, and *Fallen Angel*.

Dear Mr. Howard Fast,

I have just finished your book *April Morning*. It fascinated me how much it was like my life. Not that I was in a battle, but in the things Adam is going through, trying to prove to his parents and himself that he is more than just a boy, but a man.

It seems to me that I am constantly trying to show my dad that I can do anything he does and just as well. Mostly it's just in sports: baseball, hunting, swimming, and wrestling. I think I am, in this way, without really knowing it, trying to win his affection. And just once I would like for him to say, "That was an excellent grab at second base," "A beautiful pin, Chris," "That was a hard but well-executed shot." This is my dream—for him to acknowledge my accomplishments before that day that I see him go. Most of the time, it's, "Come on, you know you can do better than that." I think this is the way both Adam and I would like our dads to be, to act, and to feel. Deep down I know that he loves me a lot. I just can't help to wonder, Why doesn't he show his emotions?

Another way Adam and I seem to be the same is our grandmothers and the way they always refer to the Bible in any argument. My grandmother talks down to me and preaches about how there are so many bad things in this world. She is quite old now and has been through a couple of heart attacks. When grandparents tell us these things, we may not quite understand or even agree with what they say, but in the end it all usually comes true. Adam, I think, feels the same way toward his grandmother.

My mom seems to think I am still a child and not in tune with the world today. I am not free to make my own choices most of the time. It may just be that she doesn't want to let her first child grow up, as do all mothers. One night after I got into an argument with her over going out with some of my high-school friends, I was going upstairs when I overheard my dad talking to her on how she has to let go. Too bad none of it sank in—she still treats me the same ever since then. Adam's mom is the same about the battle at Lexington with the British Redcoats. It's not so much that they want to be mean, but that they care about us so much that they worry about what could happen.

I'll conclude this letter and just say thanks for helping me not to give up when I think all is lost, to keep going no matter what. Thank you, Mr. Fast.

Chris Harris, 15
Les Bois Junior High School, Boise, ID
Teacher: Dan Prinzing

Ellen Bass is a nationally recognized counselor, lecturer, and professional trainer, who has been working with survivors of child sexual abuse for more than fifteen years. She is the co-editor of *I Never Told Anyone*. **Laura Davis** is a nationally recognized workshop leader and expert on healing from child sexual abuse. She is the author of *The Courage to Heal Workbook* and *Allies in Healing*. They both live in Santa Cruz, California.

Dear Ellen Bass and Laura Davis,

In the midst of this vast world, I have learned that I am not alone. *The Courage to Heal* has given me the strength to pull myself together and go on with my life. I thought I was the only one who still cringed at bumps in the middle of the night. I felt like there was something wrong with me because I can't stand for people to touch me. I thought wrong. There are a number of women out there who are just like me. They suffered from the same trauma I suffered from; molestation and rape are all too common to ignore.

Some call your book "The Survivor's Bible," and to an extraordinary extent, it is. Although *The Courage to Heal* cannot give me the love I need, it does give me the hope that there is a better future. The hope that I will be able to sleep through a night without waking up in a cold sweat.

My molestation has scarred my soul so deeply that I chose my lifetime career to be a child psychologist. My tears will not stop rolling until I know that I have done all that I can to help those other little girls who have had to feel the misery I felt.

No matter how many times my therapist tells me it was not my fault, the little girl inside of me still blames herself. Just reading the stories of all those women eases the pain, and maybe one of these days with the help of your book, that little girl inside of me will be at peace with herself. I thank you with all of my heart for *The Courage to Heal.*

Lula Jones, 18
Flour Bluff High School, Corpus Christi, TX
Teacher: Mrs. McConell

One of the most popular novelists of this century, **John Steinbeck** was born in 1902 in Salinas, California. During his life, he worked as a painter, ranch hand, laboratory assistant, fruit picker, construction worker, and wartime correspondent for the New York *Herald-Tribune* before penning many novels. He died in 1968. Ann Marie Holmes wrote this letter in memory of her parents. Two other students' letters are in "The Power of Conviction" and "Self-Discovery."

Dear Mr. Steinbeck,

I have just completed your book *Of Mice and Men*, and I would like to share with you the tremendous effect it had on me. I identify so closely with Lenny and George, because many of their experiences mirror my own.

Last year, I lost my mother to cancer, and the year before that, my father died of a heart attack. I have felt very lost since they have gone. I feel very much like George must have felt when he had to deal with many of Lenny's problems. I know how hard it is to take care of someone you love who is dying slowly before your eyes. I did that for three months before my mother finally died.

I'm seventeen now and I chose to live on my own so I can stay in town and graduate with my schoolmates. I'm a little like Lenny, who always said he was going to live alone in a cave and take care of himself. That's exactly what I'm trying to do. I don't want to have to rely on anyone, like George, who will remind me of all the things they could be doing if they didn't have to take care of me.

I can really identify with the money issue involved in this story. Money is tight when you are just starting out on your own. I work very hard at a little part-time job, but there are so few hours I can work during the week while also attending school. I scrape to save for gas money and groceries. I can't afford ketchup, just like George and Lenny. I try to do without like they did, but I complain about it considerably more.

It's hard to go from having every need and want catered to, to going it alone. This is a choice I made. You have reminded me that this is not going to be easy, but I can accomplish my goal if I keep on trying.

Lenny and I seem to get into trouble unintentionally. I always seem to do things that other people think is wrong, and I just don't understand why. Your book opened my eyes. You have taught me to think more closely about how my actions will affect others.

They survived together because of their friendship and perseverance. They did the best they could, which is all any of us can do. I want to be a survivor like George. I also hope to be as good-natured as Lenny was and not let the world turn me cold and mean.

I want to thank you for writing this book. I needed someone to remind me that I can really make my life work if I quit feeling sorry for myself and do something about it. I needed you to help me grow up.

Ann Marie Holmes, 18
Ubly Community High School, East Lansing, MI
Teacher: Ms. Nancy Elliot

Spencer Johnson was born in 1938. He earned his medical degree from the Royal College of Surgeons in 1968, but decided he would be of more service to people through the written word. He is the author of the Valuetales series for children (e.g., *The Value of Patience: The Story of the Wright Brothers* and *The Value of Imagination: The Story of Charles Dickens*), the One Minute series for adults (e.g. *The One Minute Manager*, *The One Minute Father*, and *The One Minute Mother*), *Peaks 'n' Valleys*, and *Who Moved My Cheese?*

Dear Spencer Johnson:

I would like to thank you for writing *The Precious Present*. This is a book that has changed my whole life forever! Not only do I think it is important for everyone to learn the message it teaches, but I think that, in a certain time in my life, I was the one who needed it most!

The whole year was like being caught up in a horrendous tornado! The pieces of my life started splintering at about fourth grade. That was the year that I found out I had a serious medical problem. One minute I was playing kick ball in my yard, and the next minute I was waking up in the emergency room, not sure of anything. I was only nine years old and wasn't ready for what I was about to go through. I went to many different doctors, one at a time, but not one of them could find an answer.

I was put on many different drugs, with terrible side effects. One of the first drugs I had made the walls go in and out. Everywhere I looked something would charge at me and then run away again. Then I tried another drug, hoping it would work, but it didn't. Drug after drug I tried, calling for an answer, but it still didn't come to me. Some drugs would control my emotions. I could be really happy at one point, and then, like a bolt of lightning without a storm, I'd feel sad and depressed. I would start crying for no reason.

I missed more than half of the year at school. If I wasn't there, I was either in the nurse's office, at home, or in the hospital. It was all very overwhelming! I had lost the precious present that I had once had when I was younger. I used to always be cheerful and happy! I always tried hard to see the good things in life. But that was when I was younger, before the storm had hit.

Now the precious present had left. It had gone, far far away and I wondered if I would ever find it again. As time went on, things got worse! I couldn't seem to figure my life out. Everywhere I turned things looked bad. I was living my worst nightmare. Nothing seemed right to me anymore. It just didn't make sense. Just when I thought the storm would calm down, dark clouds gathered above me and the lightning struck again. The drugs I was on made my hair fall out and my scalp got sore! I was like a tiny, little boat at sea in the middle of a storm, with no control over which way to go. My life was like a dart board, with darts shooting at it nonstop. What had I done to deserve this?

At that point, I began to fall into my own little world. My land was clearing fast. All the trees that once stood beside me when I needed an apple had wandered away, and the stars that I had once wished upon had disappeared. My friends were gone and I had almost lost hope of an answer. I felt all alone and lost in my empty little world. I couldn't quite catch where my life was going. I wasn't sure what to do or which way to turn. As a nine-year-old child, I actually thought the next road was death.

As time went on things got better. I did much better in fifth grade. I was in school more, too. But still I couldn't get my mind off of what I had been through. I was scared at the thought of what had happened, and even more scared at the thought of it happening again!

All year I'd worry about my future with my medicine. I felt like I was wasting half my life worrying. I made some new friends and felt like part of the world again. But still, something was bothering me about my life. It wasn't a side effect of a pain. I guess it was just the thought of being scooped back up in the tornado and living fourth grade over again.

This feeling went on through the summer and the beginning of sixth grade. Then I received your book, *The Precious Present*. I loved the way it was the message it told! Then, I thought for a minute, I was just like the young man in the story. There I was, wasting my life, worrying about something that might never happen. I might as well enjoy the precious present while it lasted. And so I did. Slowly, time passed and I began to feel like my cheerful, positive self again. It felt wonderful!

The man who had once had a heart full of joy had used his life searching across deserts and through the world for just one thing. He never even thought to stop and see all the good things in his life, and enjoy the present!

I am very thankful that I had a chance to read your story, or my life could have been a disaster! I am now thirteen years old, and we haven't found an answer yet (though we will soon), but I still enjoy life as it is and get a lot out of it!!

I would like to thank you once again for writing such a fabulous story! I encourage all my friends and family to read *The Precious Present.* I now read this book over and over again. And each time I read it, it is just as great as the last reading was! I will never forget what this book taught me and how it changed my whole life—forever!

Nicki M. Schulze, 14
Elmbrook Middle School, Brookfield, WI
Teacher: Miss Dee Vradnicek

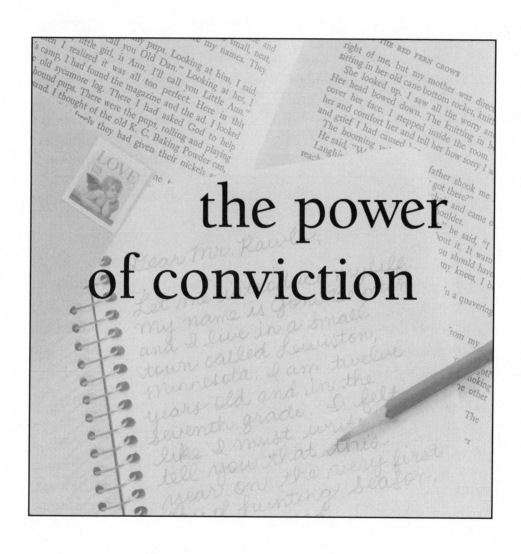

the power
of conviction

Alex Haley is the author of, among other works, the Pulitzer Prize-winning book *Roots*. He died in February of 1992. A letter about *Roots* appears later in this chapter.

Dear Mr. Haley,

"Who was Malcolm X?"

The entire eighth-grade English class sat silent at Mrs. Pfeiffer's question. I didn't have a clue. Nobody seemed to. We listened to the heater hum, and if it had been a scene from a cartoon, we would have heard crickets.

Then a dapper black friend of mine raised his hand and explained. "You know how Martin Luther King Jr. wanted blacks to be nonviolent? Malcolm kind of told them to fight back if necessary."

That was it. That was my introduction to Malcolm X. The movie and the T-shirts were still years away, there was no hype surrounding him, and yet, something intrigued me about this man. At first, I was horrified at my friend's response, amazed that there was actually a black man who told blacks to fight back against whites. Who would say such a thing?

Two years passed. My mother died, and my father and I were on poor terms. I didn't feel like going on. I thought I didn't have much chance for future success. I was Indian and Muslim, and everybody knows how Americans feel about those who are different. You are an outsider. A stranger. Nobody wants you. You can make as many white friends as you want, but when it comes right down to it, they're American; you're not.

All of those feelings changed after I read your book.

The wound of my mother's death was still sore. I needed somebody—something—to tell me that my life wasn't over. That my mother, with all of her ideals and her outlandish behavior, was not crazy. That she was a normal human being. I didn't think Malcolm had *anything* to do with her. I was wrong.

Malcolm X was so like my mother and like what I strive to be, it astonished me. Here was a man who was so different from everybody, so defiant and so honest, that whether or not people liked him became irrelevant. They *respected* him. He was a Muslim in a time when nobody had ever heard of Islam. He was an ex-con who fooled scholars into thinking he had a college education, just by reading books. And, most of all, he was honest and had the strength to change when he knew he was wrong.

Suddenly, everything my mother had told me about honesty, doing well in school, and not following the crowd had new meaning to me. Malcolm derived his strength purely from the knowledge that he was doing the right thing. He had unquestioning confidence in himself, and all the things that made me an outcast were his strengths. He was a Muslim. He changed the word from meaning "that weird foreign religion" to "watch out for those guys. They have ATTITUDE." Malcolm X would tell the whole world to kiss his ___. Well, he wouldn't say it that way. He believed that foul language was for those who couldn't express themselves. After getting out of prison, he played by the rules and never broke a law again, but he could provoke more anger from society than a mass murderer.

But the thing that touched me the most about Malcolm is how, behind this tough demeanor, he really was a normal, nice person. He knew when he was wrong; he always searched for the truth. He lived a clean life under Allah's teachings, even if those teachings cost him his own life. That's a martyr. That's a hero.

You can't measure the amount of strength I got out of your book, Mr. Haley. It's something I feel even as I walk down the street. I realize now that I am a talented, good person, and nobody can tell me otherwise. I know that there's nothing to fear from society—you can't live your life trying to do what others tell you to do. Now I know, as my mother tried to teach me time and again before she died, that you can't go wrong with truth.

Thank you for the greatest book I have ever read, *The Autobiography of Malcolm X*.

Aslum Khan, 17
Rolling Meadows High School, Rolling Meadows, IL
Teacher: Bill Leece

Upton Sinclair was born in Baltimore, Maryland, on September 20, 1878. At the age of fifteen, he began writing dime novels to pay his way through the College of the City of New York. In 1906, he published *The Jungle,* a realistic study of the inhumane conditions in the Chicago stockyards, which aided the passage of the pure-food laws and won Sinclair wide literary recognition. Later books include *World's End* (1940); *Dragon's Teeth* (1942), for which he was awarded a Pulitzer Prize; and *Another Pamela* (1950).

Dear Mr. Sinclair:

I am a 5'10", 175-pound robust guy who plays football and ice hockey. Most people wonder how I got so big in the first place, for I am a vegetarian. I am not quite sure how this all happened, but I have never enjoyed meat. My mom told me that even as a baby I would spit the meat out when she tried to feed me. It has been quite a long time since I have had red meat, like steak, probably around eight or nine years. I have had to put up with numerous tauntings either at lunch, when I order my "veggie" cheeseburgers, or at football dinners when I pass up the spaghetti with meat sauce. My meat consumption consists of a chicken McNugget here and there or a chicken wing or taco as a dare.

People ask me all the time, "How can you live without meat?" My only reply is that I have never lived *with* meat, so it's easy. "Why don't you like it?" In response to this other popular question, I reply, "I don't know, I just don't." Most people look at vegetarians as torturing themselves, like people who give up candy for Lent. I just have never relished meat. For years I have stared at my friends as they bite into a hamburger or a taco at a fast-food joint. I cringe at the thought of what additives are included in that "meat." They just counter my scowling with a snide remark or two, such as, "Wanna come over tonight for a steak dinner?" But, most people have learned and grown to respect my eating habits over time.

After reading your book *The Jungle*, I have a renewed cause for avoiding meat. I read in wonder, most times horror, at the practices of the meat-packing companies. How when a man fell into the meat traps, he was just ground up and sent away with all the other meat. The addition of the diseased and rotten meat to the "good" meat allowed by the inspectors was horrifying. It is no wonder many people become sick, and the death of little Kristofaras occurred apparently after eating a sausage link. This book told of the secrecy of the disease-infected meat around 1906. Who knows if this same conspiracy might be in progress at this very time.

The book also deals with the troubles and struggles of the poor, something very new for me. Throughout my life, I have never had to worry where I will stay or what I will live on to the next day. I have never had to give every cent to my name in the effort to obtain the bare essentials of life. Being an average middle-class citizen, reading the story of this good-natured family thrown into the deep abyss of poverty was depressing. What makes it even more savage and horrible is that it is no less a factor now as it was then. I can still remember my glancing away from beggars as they pleaded for "just a dime for a cup of warm coffee." Now I will happily drop a quarter in the dirty Styrofoam cup of the coatless, unfortunate people. Thank you for a life-enforcing, life-changing book.

Seth Rothey, 15
Findlay High School, Findlay, OH
Teacher: Judy Withrow

Dear Anonymous Teenager,

Your story *It Happened to Nancy* about your struggle with AIDS touched my heart and made me realize that the same thing could happen to me if I'm not careful about the kinds of boys I associate with and how I take care of my body.

It was awful to think that you died because of the inhuman behavior of another human—the HIV-positive boy who raped you. I wish that I could change that, but I can't. Someday I hope that I can help other people. One of the things that I want to do is work with people with AIDS and other diseases and help scientists find a cure. When I read your book and learned about your friends and family and how they acted before and after they knew you had AIDS, it made me wonder if my family and friends would act the same way. I hope that they'd act in as caring a way as yours did.

I'm really grateful to you for deciding to have Beatrice Sparks help edit your diary so that it could be published after your death. Because your book is a diary, your writing took me inside your head and heart, day to day, even hour to hour. I was there with you, and my feelings were touched. I'm sure that it inspired other people, not just me. I've read your book more than once now, and every time I finish it, I cry, thinking about all that you had to go through. Each time I close the book, I feel closer to you. It's as if I knew you before you died, like you could have been my sister. So as a sister, I hope you are all right in heaven.

Martha Hutchins, 12
Center for Teaching and Learning, Edgecomb, ME
Teacher: Nancie Atwell

Dear Mr. Wyss,

About two weeks ago, a terrible fate befell me. It was the night before my first big swimming meet of the season, and I was over at my friend's house. His giant trampoline looked quite inviting to all the guests, and more than one person was jumping at the same time. It came my turn, and another person joined me. I attempted to forward flip at precisely the right speed, height, and just the right time. Unfortunately, my foot landed bent in the wrong direction. It wasn't until later the next day that I realized that it was a tri-fracture, multibone break. It was a miserable day.

I had to miss three days of school that week. While I lay there in the living room, I found TV to be extremely boring, so I picked up *The Swiss Family Robinson* and started reading. In my entire life, I had read only about twenty books of substantial length. I was more the sports, outdoors type. I liked to be where the action was, so you can see how desperately bored I was. However, your book transformed me. Suddenly, I wasn't bored anymore.

Though my life had gone from too much to do in too little time to too little to do in too much time, I found your book to be a wonderful and interesting escape from boredom. I didn't have to grieve about not being involved in splendid daily adventures or weekend excursions. I was right in the middle of the most thrilling and fun adventure, having the greatest experience of my life within the midst of the greatest setback anyone in my ancestral line could ever have fallen victim to. You gave me a diversion that could take my mind off of the upcoming torturous six weeks of not being able to do something as simple as walking. I loved being stranded on an island that contained a part of every land biome on Earth with every type of creature and plant that could possibly fit on one island. I adored going on great adventures through an unknown wilderness with a rifle by my side, and I admired being able to start my own colony with my family as my only support. The only time that I disliked your book was when I was finished; I was angry that I could not travel back in time to when the Robinson family existed.

After reading your book, I was heartbroken, because I knew there is no more land like that which you described, no adventures quite like yours and mine. It made me think about why this had to be. The human population must reproduce itself, but why must it grow so fast? If all of our frontiers have disappeared, what's stopping humans from abolishing all the rest of any type of rugged land that Mother Earth had originally created? It seems like the few wild refuges and preserves left are in danger of becoming extinct, and with their extinction comes much greater consequences than any extinct animal. The Native Americans would never let this great continent be like this.

Of course, I could be overestimating the problem. We do, in fact, still have all of northern Canada and Australia and other less densely populated areas, but what about the great forest lands of the United States? Those are the lands that I miss the most. The rain forests are incredibly great refuges, but we're killing so much of them. I'm always asking myself, "Why must our race kill all of the land that is what the Earth originally looked like?" Can't we just hold back a little, and let the population thin out? What if we left the cities for a while and let the great forests of centuries ago grow back? If I could be president, that is what I would work so hard to accomplish.

Mr. Wyss, you've filled my mind with such a love for Mother Earth. I never want the adventure of traveling into a new frontier to become lost in a great sea of human culture. I want my grandchildren to know what it's like to live with only the land as their shelter, food, and clothing. Mr. Wyss, you have certainly succeeded in making an incredibly sad environmentalist out of me. Your work is definitely one of the strong outcries against pollution and overpopulation I have ever seen, heard, or read in my entire life; what is contained within your book is an entire world that our self-centered race has taken up in its massive hand and squeezed to a cruel and unneeded death.

Mark Mattox, 14
Portage Northern High School, Portage, MI
Teacher: Mrs. Mindy Wines

Janet Oke has written many books, including *A Bride for Donnigan, They Called Her Mrs. Doc, Heart of the Wilderness, Love's Enduring Promise,* and *The Measure of the Heart.* She and her husband live in Calgary, Alberta.

Dear Janet Oke,

Your book *The Calling of Emily Evans* affected me in a serious way. As you know, she had a calling from God to be a missionary for Him. That is what affected me the most—the missionary part. But in a different way. I'm only thirteen, so you know I could not do exactly what Emily did and stay in one place forever. So here's my story. . . .

Over this past summer, a friend of mine and I went to Mexico on a short-term mission trip. We went with our Youth Group leader and were there for a week. It was great and we had so much fun! We had a Vacation Bible School in the morning and did repair work on houses in the afternoon. The city was very poverty-stricken. It was sad, but the children were so joyful and giving with what they had. When I got home, I thought about it constantly. And I still do.

Last Sunday at church, we had a special speaker. He had been a missionary for about a year in Austria. And I thought, Hey, I want to mission in Austria! I started to think about it and daydream about it in church. As soon as I turned my attention to the speaker again, he said, "Maybe God has a special place for you in mission work." And do you know what my thoughts were next? This is like *The Calling of Emily Evans*, only it's the calling of Lacey Murphy! I was supposed to be in the nursery that Sunday morning, but my friend traded with me. I think that was a sign from God, like He really wanted me there that day. In a way, He was uncovering my path of life for me.

You know the part where Emily runs to the altar, crying because she wants to be a missionary for God? That's how I feel. I want to do things and go places for God. I remember how happy those children in Mexico were that we were there to teach them about God and how much He loves us. I want to do it again! I want to see those faces and know how happy they will be. Of course, I know there will be rejection, but that will make me want to work harder and it will make me more determined to teach them the Word and gospel of Jesus.

The other part in the book that really jumped out at me was where Nicky died and Sophie rejects Emily and her religion from her life. That made me so sad! And, in a way, it made me mad at God for letting Nicky die. It showed me how much faith you have to have in God and what He can do for you. I just loved it when Sophie's child said, "Mommy, do you think God took Nicky away from us so we would want to go to heaven and see him?" That part really made me think about the love of God.

Lacey Murphy, 14
Alden Community School, Alden, IA
Teacher: Mrs. Annabel Meyer

Henry (Hank) Aaron was raised during the Depression in Mobile, Alabama, in the Deep South. He broke into professional baseball as a cross-handed slugger and shortstop for the Indianapolis Clowns of the Negro American League. His career took him to the World Series with the Milwaukee Braves. Later he broke Babe Ruth's home-run record. Aaron hit 715 home runs in his career—a feat that was recently voted the greatest moment in baseball history.

Dear Mr. Aaron,

    I am an avid baseball fan, and really enjoyed your autobiography. Unlike a lot of the sports autobiographies I have read, *I Had a Hammer* was more than a compilation of humorous anecdotes. It documents an important part of American history. In my opinion, the civil rights movement is the most important historical event of the twentieth century. You give a very interesting perspective of the events that occurred during that time.

    You mentioned that you wanted to be a ballplayer from the time you saw Jackie Robinson play. I have felt the same way ever since I saw Ozzie Smith and the Cardinals play in the World Series in 1987. I do not have the natural talents God blessed you with, and I realize that my dream will probably not come true, but I will not give up on it. That is something your book taught me—don't ever give up your dreams.

Before reading your book, I always thought you were a bitter man with a chip on your shoulder. You always seemed to be ripping baseball in all your interviews. I couldn't believe that a man whom baseball had been so good to, had made rich and famous, could talk so badly about it. After finishing the book, I realized how wrong I had been, and I now have a great deal of respect for you. The things you and other black players went through then were both horrible and ridiculous. Your book made me realize that the integration of baseball didn't end with Jackie Robinson and still isn't over today. Your integrity and courage in the face of constant racial adversity during your baseball days have inspired me to keep plugging for a major-league contract, even though I come from a small town and will probably never get a chance to play in front of a major-league or even a college scout. I thank you for that.

I would also like to thank you and all the other black pioneers who worked diligently and courageously to integrate baseball at every level, so fans could enjoy all the great black players who have come and gone in baseball history. I can't imagine what the game would be like without them.

Chris Maize, 16
Dadeville High School, Daleville, MO
Teacher: Kim Chism-Jasper

Dear Niccolo Machiavelli,

I have recently read your most famous work *The Prince*. I thought it was an excellent book and it has broadened my view of politics and power quite a bit.

I have always had an interest in politics, following all the elections and what the elected officials did. I have also had a slight interest in becoming a politician. After I read your book, that interest was gone.

What convinced me that politics was not for me was the manner in which you said the politicians were supposed to treat the people. I know morally that I could not attempt to fool or misguide the people I was serving, like you suggested in the book. Also, the many difficulties a politician has to deal with, for little reward, has scared me away from being a politician.

I know that you wrote this book for a sixteenth-century Italian dictatorship, but the principles are basically true for this twentieth-century American democracy. If you looked through Congress today you would find too many people thinking, "Will this be popular?" and not enough people thinking, "Will this help our country?" Yet, according to you, you have to ask, "Will this be popular?" in order to be successful enough to ask, "Will this help our country?" many times.

Since I read your book, I have noticed that recently politicians have become horrible people in the eyes of the public. I believe the public is wrong. Great people or horrible people, politicians are the same people they were five hundred years ago.

Niccolo, I believe your views in this book are right, and that is exactly why I cannot become what you were, a politician.

Bill Campbell, 14
Whittier Middle School, Flint, MI
Teacher: Dr. Dorothy Sample

Michael Crichton (rhymes with "frighten") was born in Chicago in 1942 and was educated at Harvard College and the Harvard Medical School. His novels include *The Andromeda Strain, The Terminal Man, Eaters of the Dead, Jurassic Park*, and *Rising Sun*. He is also the author of four works of nonfiction: *Five Patients, Jasper Johns, Electronic Life*, and *Travels*. Among the movies he has directed are *Westworld, Coma*, and his own, *The Great Train Robbery*.

Dear Michael Crichton,

You may very well be my favorite author of all time, but it is a little early to tell, since I'm only thirteen.

I enjoyed all your books, but the one that I regard as best, ironically, is one of your older works called *A Case of Need*. I can especially identify with the narrator, Dr. John Berry, a pathologist at a hospital in Boston. His life is what I love—people and mystery. Is the tumor malignant? He knows. Is the nurse stealing morphine ampoules from the pharmacy? Dr. Berry knows.

The book attacked views that I had taken for granted in life. I don't approve of testing products on animals, but what if we hadn't? Perhaps cars wouldn't be so safe, or if we missed with our hairspray, it would blind us.

Your book has helped me to decide to become a doctor, probably a pathologist.

You were way ahead of your time when you wrote *A Case of Need*. You were way ahead of your time in all of your books. Congratulations on being my favorite writer!

Karen Ingraffia, 13
Martin J. Ryerson Middle School, Ringwood, NJ
Teacher: Mrs. Cullen

Jim Garrison was district attorney of New Orleans from 1962 to 1974. A judge of the Court of Appeals in New Orleans, he is the author of two bestsellers, *A Heritage of Stone* and *The Star Spangled Contract*, among other books.

Dear Mr. Garrison,

Three years ago, I read your book *On the Trail of the Assassins*. The subject of President Kennedy's assassination was one which had never before appealed to me. But when I began to hear the rumors of a conspiracy in Kennedy's assassination, I needed some concrete proof of a rumor that horrendous. It was difficult for my fourteen-year-old mind to conceive the United States government in that way. I quickly received more proof than I wanted.

As American citizens, we all want to believe that our government is a mothering institution. From the time of our birth, we are trained to believe that our government shelters us and keeps us safe from the rest of the world that might threaten us. The thing that takes so long for us to realize is that everything in life does not mirror the pictures that have been painted in our minds. One of the major flaws of our society is that there are very few people who will challenge what they have been taught and begin a quest for the truth. You are one of those people, and, on a smaller scale, so am I.

I began my personal quest when I began your book. While reading it, I began to ask questions of my parents, teachers, and anyone I felt would have an intelligent opinion. I asked questions about the credibility of the United States government. I gathered opinions of Kennedy's assassination, and the very fact that I asked questions on such a subject thrilled some and appalled others. By the time I finished the book, I had formed my own opinion: the government helped kill Kennedy.

For a freshman in high school, this type of realization can be shocking. It is often difficult for a person to face the fact that something he had believed to be true for his entire life is, in fact, just a dream. People are, therefore, reluctant to change views because it requires the admission that they were wrong or that a lifelong fantasy is indeed a fantasy. Your book inspired me to challenge even *your* view on the government and the assassination.

Brad Lockard, 17
Breathitt High School, Jackson, KY
Teachers: Lavonne Hubbard and Maria Bellamy

Jerome David Salinger, born in 1919, is the reclusive author of *Catcher in the Rye, Franny and Zooey*, and *Nine Stories*. He lives in Cornish, New Hampshire. Since 1965, Salinger has published nothing, but his voice continues to speak to readers of all ages.

Dear Mr. J. D. Salinger,

When I first sat down and made myself read *The Catcher in the Rye,* I didn't think I would be moved by it, but guess what? I was. Don't you hate it when people act like they're affected by something and they are really just lying about it? Like those people who are asked to write a paper on what a book meant to them and they crank out some really sappy paper just to impress their English teachers, and you know, just plain know, that they are truly not affected. This is not a phony letter—I can guarantee that. This is the real thing. No lies. To tell you the truth, that scares me a little. How could I be changed by a piece of literature? Well, I can be and I was.

I am almost exactly like Holden Caulfield. I'm opinionated. I can have a big mouth at times, and believe me when I tell you that, just like Holden, I have a low tolerance for "see-through" people. It is so hard to find a real, "true-like" kind of person. Since it is so hard to find these people, I admire that quality in a person when I am looking for friends.

When I was younger, I had a hard time expressing my individuality and being myself with people other than my friends and family. This was because I had a feeling that no matter what I did, it wasn't ever going to be as good as what anyone else did. I was a chubby little girl whom a lot of people liked to pick on. My only experience with people, besides my friends and family, were ones of hurt and suffering. Experiences like being picked last for every team or being the last one to finish running in gym class are painful memories. I'm smart in school and have musical talents, but in third grade that didn't matter so much when it came time to decide who came to pool parties and who didn't. I, of course, was too embarrassed to wear a swimsuit, so I did not go to those parties. These experiences have shaped my life in many ways, some for the better and even more for the worse. They have also made me more uncertain about myself and what others think of me.

When I read about Holden and his situation of being an outcast and kicked out of school, I quickly understood his feelings. Some people who have read this book might think that Holden is a smart-mouth with nothing good to say about anything, but I see it as his only way to make himself feel better.

I couldn't help but wonder how you could convey all the thoughts and feelings of Holden's if you hadn't somehow experienced them yourself. Were you in fact that boyish Holden Caulfield? I can't help but feel that you were. It must make you feel good to write about yourself as if someone else were describing you. You can look at all your mistakes and decisions from a different perspective, and that perspective can help you judge your life. This is a courageous thing to do. I don't know if I could write about myself and have everyone read it. If you really are Holden Caulfield, you are not only a famous literary character, you're my hero. I admire a person who can be opinionated and say things that people don't necessarily want to hear. Someone who will stand up for himself. In my life, I have done a lot of standing up for myself, and it isn't always easy. Going against the flow isn't always fun when you are the only one.

Thank you, Mr. Salinger, for giving me another friend in Holden Caulfield.

Mary C. Muse, 14
Our Lady of Mt. Carmel School, Carmel, IN
Teacher: Patricia M. Susalla

Dear Mr. Steinbeck,

I have been told about how your novels have caused outrage and anger among the now older, conservative generation at the time they were written. My first response to the way *The Pearl* portrayed your obvious resentment of the richer societies was an angry one. You seem to put all of the problems of the poor upon the rich, and this bothered me. It made me think of all the people on welfare today and how they take advantage of it. Moments after reading this book, Mr. Steinbeck, you had succeeded in making me believe that you hold the belief that people who have earned money should just distribute it among the poor.

Then later on, as I began to look back on *The Pearl*, I started to realize how maybe the "richer society" can make breaking loose from poverty hard for the poor. The factor of an education had not really entered my mind. If

Kino had had an education, he could have handled himself better in selling the pearl and possibly have broken the poverty barrier.

I, in no way, believe in handouts. In fact, handouts and mooches anger me. If a poor man could have a chance to acquire a job and doesn't because he can get along fine on handouts, he deserves to stay at the bottom of the totem pole. It's those people that try to overcome their poverty that need and deserve help from successful people.

At a time when your ideas were not popular, you chose to write them down, even though you knew that you would face ridicule and hatred. I appreciate your honesty in your writing.

Brett Foster, 16
Willow Springs R-IV, Willow Springs, MO
Teacher: Karen Foster

> **Arthur Ashe** was born in Richmond, Virginia, in 1943. An African American, he triumphed in the all-white world of professional tennis and became one of his generation's great players. A social activist, he was involved in human rights issues, particularly opposing South Africa's policy of apartheid and the U.S. policy toward Haitians seeking asylum here. He also campaigned for AIDS-related causes, after his contraction of the disease by a blood transfusion during heart surgery became known in 1992. He died of AIDS in 1993. He is survived by his wife and daughter.

Dear Ms. Moutoussamy-Ashe:

I read your late husband, Arthur Ashe's, book, *Days of Grace* and was extremely moved by it. His book taught me many things: to stay calm and rational during conflicts I encounter, to live my life to the fullest, and to fight for the things in which I believe. Being white and thankfully not suffering from any terminal illnesses, I cannot understand what it was like for him being an African American and having AIDS.

I am an avid tennis fan and player. I loved reading what it was like for him as a member and captain of the United States' Davis Cup team. During this time, he had to deal with the fiery personalities of such players as John

McEnroe and Jimmy Connors. In this book, Mr. Ashe discussed some of the conflicts he had with these players and how he dealt with them. In every conflict, he never lost control of the anger that he may have felt toward them. He handled everything rationally and calmly. I really admire that about him.

Your husband wrote, "From what we get we can make a living; from what we give, however, makes a life," and I believe that he is completely right. I know that happiness is more important than money, but Mr. Ashe taught me that even if I am happy, I should share my life and my happiness with others to live a full and rewarding life.

Amy C. Pflughaupt, 13
Ft. Zumwalt North Middle School, O'Fallon, MO
Teachers: Mrs. Ann Schmid, Mrs. Dana Humphrey

Lois Lowry was born in Honolulu, Hawaii, and now lives in Boston, Massachusetts. She has been a freelance writer and photographer since 1972 and has won numerous awards for her books, which include *Number the Stars, Anastasia Krupnik* and the Anastasia series, and *A Summer to Die*.

Dear Ms. Lois Lowry,

Your book *The Giver* was very thought-provoking. It made me kind of sad and confused. Usually, I read a book two or three times, but I was so upset by *The Giver* that I returned it to the library the very next day.

I've given it a lot of thought, and I see now that *The Giver* made me really angry. I couldn't understand the hero's reluctance to intervene when he saw and understood all the injustices being done in the community. It was horrible.

The truth is, the giver in the story and I have a lot in common. I hold some strong views that I really believe in, but I rarely stand up for them. I'm just too scared to stick out or to expose my ideas to criticism. I can't be angry at the giver in the story for something that I myself do.

I live in a small town in Oregon, where I see bigotry, prejudice, and discrimination every day. We also have strong [proposed anti-gay legislation] here, something I'm firmly against. Still, I'm reluctant to voice my arguments, because some adults and friends of mine have different views.

I understand now that anything I can do is better than doing nothing. My voice is only one, but one voice can sometimes be just enough. As long as I am true to myself, I have nothing to be embarrassed or ashamed about.

From now on, I'm going to take sides on things I feel strongly about and won't let others intimidate me. I've learned, like the giver, that no thing or cause is hopeless, as long as people believe in it and stand up for their beliefs.

Ginger Bandeen, 16
Warrenton High School, Warrenton, OR
Teacher: Kay Rannow

> **Leon Uris** was born in Baltimore, Maryland, in 1924. He left high school to join the Marine Corps. In 1950, *Esquire* magazine bought an article from him, and he felt encouraged to write a novel, *Battlecry.* As a screenwriter and then a newspaper correspondent, he became interested in the dramatic events surrounding the rebirth of the State of Israel. His other works include *The Angry Hills, Exodus,* and *The Haj.* He has also written many screenplays, among them *Gunfight at the OK Corral* in 1957. He lives in Aspen, Colorado, with his wife, Jill.

Dear Mr. Uris,

How the heck are you? I am doing all right. I have something very important to talk to you about. I want to tell you how moved I was when I was reading your book *Trinity.* I have also read *Mila 18* and *Armageddon.* All three books were great. I love how you make a historical event into a heart-warming struggle between overbearing evil and the courageous good. All your books use the good in all people to make your stories personal and true to life. That personal basis for your stories makes history enjoyable, and that in turn makes me want to learn more about the events that took place before I was born.

I can relate to the peasants in the *Trinity* book in many ways. Like them, I am growing up in a farming village, I am Catholic, and I too feel the pressures of a foreign rule. The major difference is that my foreign rule is my parents and the teachers who grew up in a different world. They do not understand the pressures that a teen today feels. The biggest problem in their days was getting sent down to the principal's office. My problems include trying to juggle work, school, music, and friends. There is peer pressure for drinking, smoking, chewing, dipping, snuff, drugs, cheating, and sex. Every day we teens are confronted with these, and each time we must refuse to give in to the temptation.

That is what Conor Larkind did. He refused to give in to the British pressure to become a nobody, and decided to become someone someday. He labored long, hard hours at the blacksmith's, went home for chores, then read and studied by lamplight. He did all the things that I am doing right now. As I read on, I could see that all his hard work was not in vain. He did become somebody and he stood up for what he believed in all his life; and even up to the point of death, he did not back down on his morals. That is how I want to be. I want to have the same strength and determination that Conor had. He makes an almost perfect role model for all of us to follow.

There are not many people you can look up to in this world. Everybody today has an angle or a gimmick. It seems that there are no more honest people in the world. Then we can open up your book to that time when honest people did exist. Where people said what they meant and meant what they said. It was a time of greater innocence. I can only pray that the world tomorrow is more like that. We all need some more innocence in our life.

I would like to thank you for writing books like *Trinity, Mila 18,* and *Armageddon*. They show us how other people succeed at odds that are even greater than our own. You have also taken some "dry" history and shown us that what happened before is not just names, places, and dates, but people and feelings. Thank you for providing that insight into world events. It may help us survive into the next century.

Jason A. Booms, 18
Ubly High School, Ubly, MI
Teacher: Ms. Nancy Elliott

Dear Mrs. Gore,

I recently read your book *Raising PG Kids in an X-Rated Society* and it had a very dramatic impact on my thoughts about the entertainment industry. I couldn't believe what you had to go through with record companies and recording artists to get your point heard. Being a seventeen-year-old high-school senior, I might be considered a "nerd" or "dork" by my peers for agreeing with you 100 percent, but after reading your book, I too think something has to be done. Kids in my generation are bombarded with images of sex, drugs, and rock and roll. Let's face it, sex sells. My question is why?

Until I read your book, my view was pretty much the same as all my friends: that recording artists should be able to sing about whatever they wanted, and it should be the public's prerogative if they wanted to buy it. After I finished your book, I realized that people were being misinformed about what they were purchasing. The sad thing is that a lot of parents don't know or don't care about the music their children are listening to.

I have bought some CDs with parental warning labels on them and I have to say that some of the song lyrics were extremely crude and vulgar. When my mother found out that I had bought CDs with labels, she made me promise not to play the songs with the controversial lyrics. At first I thought she was too strict, but after reading your book, I have decided she was looking out for my best interest. She seemed to trust me not to play the bad songs, instead of just taking those CDs away.

My eyes are now open to the fact that we live in a harsh, immoral society that thrives on images of sex and violence. I had always known that such a society existed, but I had not realized it was so close to home. I applaud your efforts to make our country aware of the consequences that can arise from young people idolizing rock musicians whose lyrics are demeaning, dehumanizing, and dangerous. Thank you for making me aware of my moral responsibility to myself, my family, and my friends.

Amy L. Horger, 17
Divine Child High School, Dearborn, MI
Teacher: Marnie Baron-Klask

> Prize-winning author **Alex Haley** also collaborated with Malcolm X on *The Autobiography of Malcolm X*—see page 48.

Dear Alex Haley,

For nearly all my life, I've wanted to be a writer—for years, I've dreamed about seeing a book with my name on the cover, topping the bestseller list. I've had plenty of encouragement, praise, and backslapping from teachers at school and at writing workshops. It seemed like everyone believed in me.

But one thing was missing—I wasn't *trying.* I could write as many poems and stories as I wanted, and talk about being a writer when I grew up, but I never realized that I couldn't wait until I grew up. Then one day I was looking through my mother's dusty old romance novels when one book caught my eye. This one didn't look like a romance! I was pretty sure that I'd heard of it, too. It had one huge word looming on the cover in block letters: *ROOTS.*

So I asked my mom about it. She said, "That book? I got it in college; I don't think I even finished it." So naturally I was interested and decided to read it. Sure enough, I found her bookmark around page 100.

Then, after a few weeks of cheering (and sometimes crying) for Kunta, Chicken George, and all the rest, I read about how the book had come to be. I was awed to find that you taught yourself to write in the navy. It seemed to be a strange time to start, but I guess it worked, because *Roots* is as smooth in every way.

But what really woke me up was when I read about your piles of rejection slips, and the long, hard road that brought you to this book. I almost slapped myself for thinking that I had time to waste. When was I going to seriously write? When I was forty?

So I set to work with a vengeance, as though any odds against me were enemies. And guess what's happened to all of my attempts so far? Rejected! I've found out that most places don't send rejection slips, but that's okay. I write my own as a reminder.

Rejection can be bitter, but when I think of you, it's also sweet. So this is what it's really like, I think to myself, and say, thank you for what your book taught me: You can't wait for something to happen to you. You have to get out there and make it happen. Your story gives me the courage to face the adversity and try again.

Brooke Sherrard, 13
Howard Junior High, Centerville, IA
Teacher: Connie Steinbach

Martha Morrison, M.D. was brought up in a typical middle-class Southern Baptist home in Fayetteville, Arkansas. The shadow of drug addiction crept into her life at the age of twelve. Today, she is the director of a major addiction recovery team in Atlanta, Georgia.

Dear Dr. Morrison,

    I am a seventh grader at Jinks Middle School who was interested in reading a book on someone's life. I went to the bookstore and looked at biographies. They all seemed pretty boring except yours, *White Rabbit.*

    I noticed as I read your book that you started out by sneaking drugs. I think this will help kids and adults realize that if they are having medical problems, they should get medical help or ask someone else about it, because it ended up as the start of your drug abuse. I understand that you began sneaking drugs for relief of the headaches and pains you had. I realize that kids also sneak drugs for the quick high. Seeing how the sneaking began your drug addition, I understand that I must not sneak one beer or one pill. The only thing that can work for me will be to say no to drugs.

    I noticed that just about everything you did was related to friends. This has made me see how important it is to choose the right friends, because peer pressure influences many people. I see through your example how I must make my own decisions and not follow my friends.

Your book showed me how a drug addict can hit a low to the point of attempting to commit suicide. This has shown me how drugs can affect the outlook you have on life. I enjoy life and will not take any drug that would make me want to end my life.

This book impressed me so much that I did an oral report on it in the hope that I could share with other people that what you did was wrong and not to do it. My classmates seemed to be impressed with your experiences, and I hope it changed their attitudes, too. As I, and other people who have read your book, go into the world and face what you faced, I hope we will remember you and your problems, because anyone can say yes, but it takes someone strong to say no.

You were very fortunate that you overcame your drug addition and became a successful doctor. I understand that not all drug addicts are so fortunate to kick their drug habit out the window. No is the only answer I can give for drugs.

Thank you for sharing your experiences with me and other teenagers so we can learn through your mistakes and eliminate drug abuse in our lives.

Jeremy Longshore, 13
Jinks Middle School, Panama City, FL
Teacher: Mrs. Burgans

Dear Alan Paton,

"Yet men were afraid, with a fear that was deep, deep in the heart, a fear so deep that they hid their kindness, or brought it out with fierceness and anger, and hid it behind fierce and frowning eyes. They were afraid because they were so few. And such fear could not be cast out, but by love . . . ."

With these words I read the final pages of *Cry, the Beloved Country,* closed the book, and then sat there, quiet and deep in thought. I was tired. I felt as if I, too, had gone on the journey that Stephen Kumalo had traveled in his search to restore his family.

Your novel opened my eyes to a world completely alien to me: the world of South Africa. What did I know of the injustices of apartheid, how unfeasible success is for a black man in Johannesburg, what a different crime it is for a black man to kill a man who was white as opposed to black? To all this I was ignorant. The world I live in today is so tremendously different from South Africa. Yet I feel that after reading your novel, I have been given a firsthand account of the plight of South Africa as well as the beauty of its land. Through the eyes of Stephen Kumalo, I felt his pain and frustration in seeing his land and his people slip away and in the derogatory treatment he received from others. I understand now the struggles of the blacks and others in South Africa to find a voice in the government and in their fight to equalize living conditions and rights with whites.

Your novel taught me that love has the ability to break through even the strongest of walls. Love surpasses differences in color, age, and money; it overcomes the fieriest pride, the deepest hatred. To read of the acts of kindness in your novel showed me the capability of human compassion in today's world that is so darkened by greed, competition, and anger.

Before reading your novel, I had believed that the only way to get ahead was to fend for yourself and yourself only. Growing up in today's world, I had already learned to doubt the trust or intentions of others; I was skeptical of the notion that humanity was good on the whole; I had forgotten what a kind word or a helping hand can accomplish in the hearts of people.

Now I realize my folly—the only way to overcome the absence of love is with an abundance of love. I understand that sometimes, behind the harsh treatment or hurtful words of others, is really fear and insecurity. Regardless of the situation, facing a person or problem with patience and determination will create a heart of strength and dignity. I always try to remember this now when tempted to yell irrationally or burst into a fit of tears when angered or frustrated with events in my life.

Cry, the Beloved Country depicted the power of the human heart and proved to me what the courage of one person can do, especially when seemingly overpowered or outnumbered. Through your writing, my eyes were opened to the struggles among the people in South Africa. I now have the desire to fight apartheid and racism and to remember that we are all of the same human race. By working together, we can accomplish projects of infinite magnitude. For teaching me this, I am forever grateful to you.

Gina Song, 15
Illinois Math and Science Academy, Peoria, IL
Teacher: Dr. Martha Regalis

Ray Bradbury was born in 1920 and worked as a newsboy in Los Angeles from 1939 to 1942, when he became a full-time writer. A member of the Science Fiction and Fantasy Writers of America, he has published more than twenty-three books—novels, collections of short stories, poems, and plays—since his first published story when he was twenty years old. His writings for children include *Switch on the Night* and *The April Witch.* For adults he has written novels including *Something Wicked This Way Comes* and *I Sing the Body Electric.* Many of his stories have been adapted to motion picture and television movies.

Dear Mr. Bradbury,

I love to read. I read all sorts of books, and they all have one thing in common: they make me happy. It's kind of a rule that I almost always follow— almost. The exception I made for your book changed me. It changed my outlook on censorship and gave me feelings on how important it is to protect every book.

Last year in English class I wanted to earn some extra credit. *Fahrenheit 451* was on the extra-credit book list, so I read it. It made me feel angry and sad. People were paid to burn books. The only person I ever heard of who burned books was Hitler. Everyone knows that he was a crazy man. I just wanted to shout, "Stop it! You can't do that! You have no right to do that!" Charging into someone's home and burning their books is wrong. Destroying the thoughts, feelings, and souls of the people who wrote those books is wrong. As I read, I could smell the smoke and see the glowing pages, and tears welled up in my eyes.

What a relief! It was just a book—nothing real. It could never really happen—or could it? I began to think about how it all started in the novel, by getting rid of one book because some group didn't like it. Then another one was gone and another, and so on, until they were all gone. Don't we have those same groups, who don't like one book or another and who feel they should be banned for some reason? Where is this taking us? One day, am I not going to be able to read a book when I go to the beach? Will my children not be able to have the joy and comfort of hearing a bedtime story? We must never let that happen.

Thank you, Mr. Bradbury, for showing me the great importance of books of all kinds and for showing me what life would be like without any books. Before I read your book, I thought that it wouldn't matter much if a few books were censored in some way or even banned altogether. Now I see where that can lead to and that it is essential to our country and our lives that we preserve the freedom of all writers. Like in your book, I can imagine our world without Shakespeare, Emerson, Robert Frost, and Dr. Seuss. It is definitely a world in which I would never want to live. For as Milton said, "Who kills a man, kills a reasonable creature, God's image; but he who destroys a good book, kills reason itself."

Shifra Wells, 18
Fowlerville High School, Fowlerville, MI
Teacher: Mrs. Dine

Maya Angelou was born in Arkansas in 1928. She attended public schools there and in California. She studied dance, music, and drama. She is an internationally renowned author, poet, and playwright, as well as a professional stage and screen performer and singer. She is the author of an autobiographical series beginning with *I Know Why the Caged Bird Sings.* Her numerous books of poetry include *And Still I Rise* and *Oh Pray My Wings Are Gonna Fit Me Well.* She has written for television and was the inaugural poet for President Clinton in 1992.

Dear Maya,

Please don't think that I am being overly familiar by addressing you by your first name. I felt close to you as I read your book *I Know Why The Caged Bird Sings,* and was sorry to reach the last page. As I sadly closed the book, I felt that I was saying good-bye to an old friend. In addition to getting to know you, I came to like and admire your whole family. I laughed when you described how fanatic your grandmother was about cleanliness. In my imagination, I could see her standing over you, demanding that you scrub harder while you shivered in that tub of cold water. I could just see her coming into your bedroom after you were asleep and looking under the covers to ensure that your feet were clean; and when she found them dirty, she would make you get up and go out into the dark to draw water from the well to rebathe. You were afraid to go to the well at night because your brother had convinced you that snakes were there, waiting for people in the dark. Your brother is a lot like mine. He enjoyed tormenting you, but he also protected you, and you loved him as I do mine.

You grew up in a poor and humble home. You were poor from a lack of money, but you were rich in other things that are so much more valuable: love, family, tradition, and closeness. You grew up without a TV or even a radio; consequently, your family depended upon each other for support and even for entertainment. You were close not only with your immediate family but also with your extended family.

American families today are fragmented and disjointed, because most families in the United States have been too mobile. They have moved too far from their roots, and because of this they have lost much of their family ties. We don't learn from our grandparents because we seldom see them. Our only contact with cousins and aunts and uncles is an occasional birthday or Christmas card. For example, I have seen my grandparents on only a few occasions, and I have aunts, uncles, and cousins whom I have never seen. Your family was always there when you needed them; and I envy you and believe that there is much to be learned from families such as yours. Although we can never go back to the pretelevision era, when families were born, grew up, lived, and died in the same community, we must, however, search for a beacon that will guide us back to the basics of life, and certainly the family unit must be the shining light of the beacon.

Your experiences of growing up in an era in which racism was so prevalent was sad and frightening. I find it frightening, because I am not so sure that we have really come very far. On the surface, it would appear that we have made progress in race relations, but I believe that the progress is very fragile. Race relations are made so difficult by the competitiveness of our society. We compete with each other for everything, and it is so easy to blame our failures on each other. It is particularly easy to blame our failures on someone who looks or speaks differently.

You mentioned that from childhood you grew up not liking white people. That makes me sad, and I hope you have changed. I would like nothing more than to walk with you to that old water well and have a cup of cold water (I always think that water tastes so much better when it comes straight from the ground; we buy ours in a bottle from XTRA) and talk about family, togetherness, and trust and about our future as a nation. Wouldn't it be nice if we were really "one nation, under God, with liberty and justice for all?" Thank you so much for sharing your life with us, and I really do understand why a caged bird sings.

Sherry Cox, 16
Antilles High School, Fort Buchanan, Puerto Rico
Teacher: L. Solís

self-discovery

Dear Mr. Hemingway:

Several weeks ago, my language arts teacher gave us an assignment that required the reading of a novel. When I mentioned the task to my dad, he went to the basement and brought me a book with a picture of a shack near the shore on the cover *[The Old Man and the Sea].*

My first reaction was to ask what the book was about. He replied, "It's a story about an old man, a fish, a Yankee, and a few other things."

"What's so special about this book?" I asked. "Why should a twelve year old read about an old man?" He gave me a look that he is famous for, and said, "Even if you don't like the story, maybe you'll learn how to catch a fish, so next time we go to Montauk, we won't come back empty-handed."

With that, my own journey began through what I thought would be a very long 127 pages. Boy was I wrong! With each page, the pieces all began to fall in place. This wasn't just a story about a fisherman, but a lesson in life!

Over the years, my dad had impressed upon me the importance of respect, something called the work ethic, and the need to look at life as a whole and not let any single event cause ups and downs. This book reinforced these values. It reinforced the belief that perseverance and determination are values that cannot be conquered by bad luck. Simple men can becomes heroes, and being a hero to yourself is as important as being a hero to others.

Most parents encourage you not to give up and to keep trying. That is certainly the case with me. My parents gave me tools, opportunity, and, most of all, their time. I learned an important lesson in your book. Reach far for your dreams, but know when to quit. Know your limitations, accept them with grace and dignity, then move on with your life.

True, the old man did catch his marlin. However, the process of life and the laws of nature took over, and the small boat could not keep the sharks from destroying the marlin. Even in victory, you can lose. One can learn that winning at the expense of something else is not a real victory. We each have a place in life, and nature's laws have to be respected.

I see how some things should not carry the importance they do. More important, I now see that character, relationships, and respect are more meaningful. Just as the old man learned his limitations and mourned the destruction of his catch, so have I learned to not only set goals, and travel great distances to capture a dream, but to know how to go about achieving them.

The symbolic old shack near the sea on the cover of your book has been able to withstand many storms, so will the valuable lessons of life in your novel.

Mark Balian, 12
George White School, Hillsdale, NJ
Teacher: Mrs. Carol Hudzik

Dear Avi,

Sailing on a ship in my imagination has taught me many significant subtleties about myself. In school, my teachers try to have me find out more about my personality by looking within. I never really could, although I pretended to. I guess you have to know of other people who make you admire their personality to reflect what yours is like. Charlotte Doyle was that person for me.

The way I see it, Charlotte was a polite girl who always did what other people wanted before she boarded the *Seahawk*. That was my personality before I read *The True Confessions of Charlotte Doyle*. I'm still polite, but now I don't let people push me around.

I love the part where Charlotte became a member of the crew. To me, that was when she decided to start letting her true self shine through. She became a braver and more self-assured person after that, and that's exactly what I'm trying to do.

One thing that Charlotte's experience let me realize was how fortunate I am. She gave me the knowledge that girls my age can be courageous and not be bothered by little worries like I have. My worries are getting to class on time, whether my hair is messed up or not, and trying to get good grades. Hers are much more serious. She had to worry about things like not getting killed! I consider myself a very lucky thirteen-year-old girl, compared to the very brave Charlotte Doyle.

I think Charlotte is an inspiration for me to find who I really am, instead of what people want me to be. I like that idea and will keep trying to listen to that little voice inside of me saying who I really am, instead of what my peers and others want me to be. Thank you for helping me with my "voyage" of discovery in my life. I promise to keep reading your books and hope to find more inspirations in my life like Charlotte.

Megan Ryan, 13
Heaton Middle School, Pueblo, CO
Teacher: Mrs. Mishmash

Dear Toni Morrison,

I own a sixteen-year-old patchwork quilt. This unified and yet diverse quilt is every book I have ever read, pieced together daintily, so as not to harm the contents.

The quilt is a prism of many colors. Yet there is one imperfection—one off-centered orange square that has a mind of its own, yet no voice. I always despised its silence, its ugliness. I longed to conquer every square, discover all secrets, unearth every tale. This orange square was my failure, I could not bear even to look at it, let alone touch it.

All the lush squares are books, but the orange patch is a particular volume, written by an African American woman. The book, the orange patch, stuck like a thorn in my side, its secrets sheathed by the shadows of a sunset on some distant horizon.

For a time I could no longer read orange books. I feared a discovery of more of my shortcomings and ignorance, yet the orange square wouldn't go away. One, two, three years, the square remained untouchable, unreachable, incomprehensible. I shoved it to the back of my shelf and turned the quilt around so that the orange square was at my feet, but I grew more perplexed, even exasperated.

Then I picked up another orange book. Maybe through it I could discover the essence of orange, this tart color that I could not taste. I wrapped my quilt around me on my bed and began to read your book *Beloved*. You let me enter the world of the black woman. You were my orange door.

Your quilt has now become my quilt, too, and I am beginning to comprehend why the "Two patches of orange looked wild—like life in the raw" (*Beloved*, p. 38).

I hope to meet you someday, in the sharp-edged light. As in your book, "we will not be holding hands, but our shadows will."

Rena Bunder, 15
RASG Hebrew Academy, Miami Beach, FL
Teacher: Arlene Fishbein

Dear Delanie Rawn,

Your Dragon Prince trilogy has taught me a bit about myself and others. The first is your ever-present, very true, if I say so myself, theme about using power. "Don't use power unless it is necessary, because each time you do, it gets easier to use again." (I am paraphrasing, of course.)

I thought about it a lot! I asked myself, "Am I doing this?" Sadly, the answer was yes. One, my tongue was/is sharp, as sharp as a katana blade. Though I rarely insult people and put them down, the times I did, it really hurt. I always thought, Big deal; I am not mean often.

Then I noticed a friend of mine and his friends. They put down and degraded people, and like the High Warlord of the Vellant'im, they used their power to the extreme. They constantly put people down, swore. They did it without even thinking about what they were doing. I realized that being mean even sometimes is too often. I would end up like the High Warlord of the Vellant'im if I continued using that power.

Also, I realized how delicate a vision is. When my parents came to this country, they had a vision. Like Rohan, they made their vision come true. I saw that my visions and dreams of sweet illusions were so delicate, so mortal. What takes years to build can be destroyed in a fraction of the time. Someone must have a vision to rebuild it, whatever it may be. On the way to achieving my goals, I will help achieve the goals of others. My vision may be besieged, but if I try hard enough, I can succeed.

A frivolous but potentially important thing I also learned about was praise. You really did a good job with Meiglan. If you do what is expected, it's normal. But when you are praised, you did something special—for you. Some people are complimented for doing simple things, but that shows how highly people think of them! I give people praise according to their ability. I hope people do the same for me. When certain teachers, friends, and my parents say, "You did well," I probably did very well and I feel pleased.

Your series has taught me so much about myself. Thank you.

Khang Nguyen, 15
Wheaton-Warrenville South High School, Wheaton, IL
Teacher: Ms. Susan McNeal-Bulak

Charlotte Brontë was born in 1816 in Yorkshire, England. Her first novel, *Jane Eyre*, became an immediate success. *Shirley* (1849), *Villette* (1853), and *The Professor* (published posthumously) are the rest of her novels. She died in 1855, a year after her marriage.

Dear Charlotte Brontë,

I am writing in regards to your book *Villette*. This book has had a large influence upon my life. Picking up your book is like wrapping in a warm blanket of familiarity. I never find it difficult to understand your character's feelings; I have experienced many of them myself. I feel somewhat akin to Lucy, perhaps because her story could just as easily be mine. At different points, Lucy's thoughts so closely mirror mine, it was eerie. Lucy dreads changes in the weather because of the odd emotions it awakens in her, yet she is drawn to storms and cannot leave until the spectacle is through. This same odd emotion is brought forth in me during a storm. Something inside me aches and will not be soothed. I, too, am drawn to watch nature's fury— the flickering sky and pounding thunder. Something won't let me leave until the rage is quieted. Yet, while Lucy is upset by this and longs for escape, I am calmed.

Her inner conflicts have, at some time, been mine. Constantly at war are feeling and reason; how many times has reason told me to ignore feeling? When Lucy insists on writing with feeling and blocking out reason, I see myself being allowed to write with unchecked emotion. Then, as Lucy listens to reason and shreds her letter, I, too, submit and write a weak, half-sincere version of the first. One is written for my own satisfaction and will live on paper only a short time. The other will continue its journey to a mailbox or a teacher's desk.

I also see myself in Lucy when she goes to her alley; she needs physical separation to truly be alone with her thoughts. I often wonder, does her heart quicken, as mine does, when footsteps approach? Does she hide, afraid that someone is come to rob her of her solitude? Or can she go on thinking as freely as before, as if someone hadn't intruded on her privacy?

In Lucy's life, I saw, at first, no wrong. How could I find fault in a nature that is so close to my own? But if I step back and detach my feelings of kinship, her faults jump out, and I see them reflected in myself. This woman lives quietly, observing life, but rarely participating. She keenly watches others and takes in their expressions—I had never fully realized what I was doing until then. I had always thought it was impolite to stare and tried to stop because it often made people fidget, but this was more than an act of boredom. She was watching others live the life she was missing. I thought of her as an anonymous biographer of life. Until I thought, am I missing life, too?

Someone once said, "A man's reach should exceed his grasp." Lucy's reach falls short of what she could grasp. Why does she settle for what she is not happy with? Does she lack motivation or courage? Seeing in her my own lack of motivation and my pessimistic attitude toward life, I decided to change things. I decided to make it my private goal to reach. I first consulted a supreme source on my future: a Magic 8-Ball. I concentrated hard on the number 8 and asked if my grimmest guesses were true. Am I doomed to become a single, old woman who smells like mothballs and gives crocheted doilies as presents? Will my only companions be the neighborhood strays? Will I be a burden on friends and family because I never got my driver's license? To these questions I always got a firm yes. This I decided was my probable future, but could it be changed? Yes, I can avoid mothballs for the rest of my life and never learn to crochet. My future is as changeable as the weather. In any situation, I am not restricted to that which I think is my destiny. I am glad that through Lucy I saw this and don't have to learn through my mistakes.

I think Lucy is a path I might take. I suppose that's a benefit of reading— it allows you to experience so much more than you can in just one life. I am glad I read your book and I will happily pass it along to my friends.

Evelina Businaro, 15
Chaska High School, Chaska, MN
Teacher: Mr. Tom Finnegan

Dear Barbara M. Joosse,

This is a special thanks for writing *[The Pitiful Life of Simon Schulz]*. My life was manifested in my mind as I read this book. Through the years from kindergarten to seventh grade, I felt I needed to just run away after years not of sorrow but of melancholy and pain. Kindergarten was but only a trailer house. I was the first child of four, and my parents didn't yet know how to act or provide me with everything I needed. Third grade began all right. I soon found out it wasn't going to stay this way.

Often, at recess I'd find myself sitting on the ledge of an impression in the wall, where the windows would slightly protrude. I wasn't able to laugh with my classmates, because when I laughed it suddenly wasn't funny anymore. I couldn't play games, because they always found a way to discourage me or get into a fistfight, all against one, where I was the one. In baseball, the ball was thrown *at* me instead of pitched. A mere slumpish walk home with my head hung low and my brother and sister behind me turned into a snowball fight. My sister gets scared easily and she was scared to the point of almost crying because of the snowballs that held rocks. There was only one ever thrown at her; it missed only to hit my patiently waiting hand that now has a permanent scar and I a personal memory.

After sixth grade was over, I thought my life couldn't get any worse. It was now the start of a three-month break before seventh grade, and I was reading books, watching TV, and sleeping. My dad loved to go to bookstores, so I went and found a book that changed the way I would think forever; it was entitled *The Pitiful Life of Simon Schulz* by Barbara M. Joosse. I liked the book, I liked the detail, and after awhile I realized that was me on the cover.

Each chapter told a different story of my life. I brought the book with me everywhere—to the grocery store, the restaurant, and on trips. I read the book [in the dark] when a car came and I leaned to the door to catch the beams of light that protruded from the headlights of each car. I finally finished and thought I should leave the past behind, remember that the future lies ahead, and that I can change the way my life's direction is heading. My life now has changed from horrible to well—who could ask for anything more. I now have a ten- and a six-year-old brother, an eight-year-old sister, a kind and loving mother and father, and some very special friends. Each and every one of them helps me with problems I face in everyday life, and so to this author, Barbara M. Joosse, I give my thanks and happiness. Now because of your book, I have a new candle with a flame burning strong, and placed beside it are five very special other ones—Bob, Donna, Logan, Meghan, and Ian. My family.

Sean T. O'Brien, 12
Hughes Junior High School, Bismarck, ND
Teacher: Mrs. Peggy Hoge

Charles Dickens was born on February 7, 1812, in Landport, Portsea, England. He worked as an attorney's clerk and newspaper reporter until his *Sketches by Boz* (1836) and *Pickwick Papers* (1837) brought him success as an author. Considered one of the greatest novelists, he died on June 9, 1870. Other works include *Great Expectations, A Tale of Two Cities,* and *David Copperfield.*

Dear Charles Dickens,

A year ago, I had the pleasure of reading *Great Expectations*. This book proved to be a very interesting account of a boy rising to success. As I got farther in the book, Pip's actions astonished me. I could not believe that Pip had become so arrogant, forgetting some of his friends and family in his rise to success.

The more I read, the more I tried to relate my life and the people around me to the life of Pip. When I was younger, I had thought that money solved every problem: If you broke the family stereo, buy a new one; if you lost your backpack, buy a new one; if you were bored, buy a new toy. I was amazed at all that money could do for a person. But one thing that I realized after reading *Great Expectations* is that money cannot buy happiness. Miss Havin-sham had an immense amount of money, but she was not happy. Money did not buy her love, either, for she was left standing at the altar.

I think this novel was telling its readers to stay true to the ones they love and to always stay loyal to friends and family, no matter what their status is in school or in the community. I have thought a lot about this, hoping that if I ever become rich and famous, I will remember the people who helped me get to where I am in life. I hope that I never look down on them as being little people.

Mr. Dickens, the main theme that I got out of your book is not to take the things I have in life for granted. I personally think that people should cherish the things that we have and never concentrate on the things that are missing in our lives. I try to catch myself whenever I start to feel sorry for myself, and try to think about how lucky I am for what I have in my life. This book has helped me to see that happiness does not have a price tag. Thanks for shedding the light and opening new ideas for me in how I treat people now and forever.

Chelsea Maddux, 15
Central High School, San Angelo, TX
Teacher: Ms. Louise Jones

Carol Matas lives in Winnipeg, Canada, with her husband and two children. She is the author of *The DNA Dimension; The Fusion Factor; Zanu; Me, Myself and I;* and the highly praised *Lisa's War.* She writes full-time and also visits schools to do readings and conduct workshops.

Dear Carol Matas,

As I read your book *Daniel's Story,* it really showed how much I cared about my family. I have lived for only eleven years, but I was truly touched by the way your book brought the true feelings of how much I love and care for them. I could not imagine losing a parent. About four years ago my grandfather died, and my life ripped apart. Yet Daniel lost someone much closer to him—his mother, the only person he knew he could count on and be with forever—but he was able to go on and be stronger.

The day I read your book was an early Saturday morning. After I finished, I then knew that I was going to be a writer. I was going to write the hopes and dreams of all. I knew I could. I wanted to give that feeling of hope and grief to children and adults. I was going to open up and give my all to make my dream come true. About a week later at school, we were assigned to write a sixteen-page story. I felt that I put a lot of effort into it. Mrs. Matas, my one wish would be to talk to you to see how you came up with Daniel, to see how a real writer does her magic. I loved your book and someday I hope to write a book as good as yours.

Ami Williams, 11
Appomattox Elementary School, Appomatox, VA
Teacher: Mrs. Kim Harvey

William Sleator is the author of many enormously popular science-fiction and suspense thrillers for young adults. His books include *The Green Futures of Tycho, Among the Dolls,* and *House of Stairs.* Mr. Sleator worked as a rehearsal pianist for the Boston Ballet company for nine years, touring with them throughout Europe and the United States. He now divides his time between his home in Boston, Massachusetts, and Bangkok, Thailand.

Dear Mr. Sleator,

Aliens and supernatural power are not only ideas, theories created by us Homo Sapiens. I believe there must be "creatures" living on other planets, and frequently argue this point with friends. I enjoy thinking about these topics. Your book *Interstellar Pig* made me think so hard, it was difficult to concentrate on anything else. I am writing to tell you my feelings about your book, my favorite. I am not going to tell you how well written or how much fun it is, because you already know that. I really want to tell you what went on in my mind as I read it and how I reacted.

The first time I read *Interstellar Pig,* I was not concentrating so much on the writing, but more on the plot and putting myself in the story. That was not hard. Even though I am a twelve-year-old girl, I felt like the main character, a teenaged boy named Barney. While Barney was meeting his new neighbors in the cabin next door, I was also greeting them. When Barney was forced into getting sunburned, I felt his pain. When he played the interstellar game, I whispered where he should move next. And when he was fighting off the three extraterrestrials, in my mind, I was helping him. My mind was actually in the book, even though my body was not. I had the same feelings that Barney did.

If I were to compare one of the characters in *Interstellar Pig* to myself, I think that Barney and I have the most in common. Sometimes he is a coward, but other times he is very brave at heart and head. Some of his actions may not have been smart, but you can understand why he made the choices he did. He is also very curious, willing to try new things, and his curiosity could have gotten him in trouble if he did not have a careful side. These are all qualities I have. I can be afraid to do something or go somewhere, but I make myself try. I am also very curious, but at the same time I am careful. And I understand the difficulty in making the right choice.

I was neither happy nor sad at the end of this book. I was amazed. I may have had a smile on my face, but it was a smile of awe. My stomach churned as I began to think back in the book. I wondered if the story could happen. I felt it really *had* happened.

When you wrote this book, you used a scientific concept—that of aliens visiting the earth. This may not be very logical right now, but it will probably happen in the far, far future. I have read other extraterrestrial books, and I have not found *any* that made me really believe in them. As soon as I read *Interstellar Pig,* it made me think about what might happen when we first confront aliens. It also made me question whether extraterrestrials would be smarter or more powerful than human beings. Would we stand a chance against them? Would we get along?

When people hear you are reading books about aliens, they cringe and think that you are reading strange, faddish books. You should be reading books about events that really happened. Some people even think that science-fiction books are for younger kids, not for a seventh grader, who should be more mature and past this stage. Your books are different. They have a realistic science basis that you expand to create a fast-paced, fun, fictitious fantasy.

This combination of science and storytelling is what impressed me the most. Without cheap thrills or horror, you mix science and good writing. I love science and I love to write, but I was not sure how to combine these two together until I read your books. When I grow up, I am going to be a science-fiction writer. But I will not write about things that have no logic at all. I will use an idea from an area of science and then combine it with a good story. I will set the scene so that readers can imagine they are there. Readers of my books will be challenged to read between the lines and learn about science. I will try to get them to enter the book, not physically but mentally. I will dedicate at least one of my science-fiction books to you.

Although *Interstellar Pig* had a fairly happy ending, at least for Barney, I was sweating all over. It was a good sweat, the sweat of seeing my future. My stomach turned and my mind was full. At that moment, I felt that I had won the game "interstellar pig."

Lindsay Renick Mayer, 12
Longfellow Middle School, Wauwatosa, WI
Teacher: Thomas Zigan

Dear Mr. Yep,

Reading *Child of the Owl* provoked thought in me. I am an American-born Chinese. When I was reading your book, I discovered I could really relate to Casey's uncle, Phil.

Like Phil, I was embarrassed about my mother's old-fashioned customs. I wanted to think of myself as being Westernized. I was embarrassed whenever my mother used my Chinese name in front of my friends. It was so uncool! I also didn't like the way my mother dressed, because she was from Hong Kong and looked like an "F.O.B." Looking like white people seemed so cool. They wore trendy clothes; had beautiful blue, gray, or green eyes; and red, brown, or blond hair. My family had only dull brown eyes and plain black hair. My mom seemed weird and too superstitious. She made me bring rice and strange Chinese food to school for lunch. I remember looking at the other girls' sandwiches. I was always longing to be different from my Chinese culture in every way I could. I thought being like the white girls made me cool and one of the crowd.

It wasn't until I read your book that I thought differently. Paw-Paw and Casey's relationship made me see how special it is to be Chinese. It was the factor that made me an individual. I saw that everything I did with my family, from ancestor worship to sharing a Chinese-style dinner, was as special as white people, because of the honor and love my culture stands for. Now I understand why my mother prayed to my ancestors with me, spoke Chinese to me, and told me traditional folktales—to keep my culture alive and flourishing in me, and to help me learn to love my people. She is like Paw-Paw because she told me stories and taught me how to use the talents hidden in me. I longed to be special, which is what my mother made me.

Betty Chu, 12
St. Gabriel School, San Francisco, CA
Teacher: Ms. Lynn Grier

Paula Danziger is a former junior-high school teacher, who now writes full-time. She is the author of many bestselling novels for young adults, including *Can You Sue Your Parents for Malpractice?*, *The Divorce Express*, *It's an Aardvark-Eat-Turtle World*, and *Everyone Else's Parents Said Yes*. She lives in New York City.

Dear Paula Danziger,

I first read *The Cat Ate My Gymsuit* as a reading assignment. Then, somewhere along the line, I got into the book.

I sometimes feel like Marcy. I think I'm fat, but I'm as skinny as a toothpick. I wear glasses. They make me not look so attractive. Once in a while I feel rejected. Then I come to my senses and realize I'm a great person. I think that was Marcy's problem. She didn't have any faith in herself.

Paula, your book has taught me a lot. One, being beautiful isn't everything. Two, don't be afraid to stand up for what you believe in. I have trouble with that one. I'm really shy. I'm working on it, though. And three, I'm very lucky to be me. I wouldn't want to be Marcy and have a verbally abusive father. Your book has changed me. It made me want to share my own feelings.

Sinoun Hooper, 12
Minnetonka Middle School East, Minnetonka, MN
Teacher: Ms. Bonnie Harnit

In 1966, **Ellen Raskin** gave up a successful career as a freelance artist to write and illustrate children's books. Her first book was the popular *Nothing Ever Happens on My Block*. Fifteen picture books followed, including *Spectacles* and *Twenty-two, Twenty-three*. As her fans grew up, so did her books. *The Mysterious Disappearance of Leon (I Mean Noel)* was her first full-length novel. Then came *Figgs and Phantoms*, a Newbery Honor Book; *The Tattooed Potato and Other Clues;* and now *The Westing Game*. She lives and works in an old brick house in New York City.

Dear Ellen Raskin,

It all started in my classroom when we were going to read a book entitled *The Westing Game*. The assignment at the time struck me as boring, because I figured the book would be a family adventure or science fiction. But I was not aware that behind the title page was something that would change my perspective on reading and writing forever. I became addicted to every word, every page. The outside world suddenly meant nothing to me as I entered a new, make-believe world that allowed my imagination to be set free by taking me away from all the drab and dreariness to a place alive with excitement and intrigue.

Mr. Hou, the cook. When he was first introduced, his bad temper and grouchiness made me suspect him of murdering Mr. Westing. But later I found out I was tricked, because he was quite innocent. This brought to my attention the question of whether or not we could be this misled in real life. Since human feelings are fragile and easily bruised, I decided I would from now on make the effort to walk the extra mile and get all the facts before I wrongly accuse someone of something they may not have done.

In the past year, I have noticed pieces of the book in various places in my life. One big example is a short mystery I wrote after reading the book, *Waiters, Guitarists and Hosts, Oh My!* The idea of creating a mind-boggling puzzle for others to enjoy was so exciting to me. Not only could I get others to stretch their imaginations, but it also gave me a chance to be as creative as I pleased in bringing a bunch of silly words to life. Now after personal experience, I think I understand what gives such oomph to writing: the need to hear children laugh, the need to know confused minds are working on solutions to problems, and especially the need to encourage someone to pick up that pen and paper and create a world of their own, like you encouraged me. And for this same reason, if you're walking down the aisle in the library someday, and you happen to see a book on the shelf with my name on it, just remember this letter I sent to you and you'll figure out the reason why it's there.

Robin Jebavy, 13
Elmbrook Middle School, Brookfield, WI
Teacher: Mrs. Karen Pappas

Dear Dr. Seuss,

As I grew up, I enjoyed reading a lot of your books, especially *The Cat in the Hat* and *Green Eggs and Ham*. These books were both enjoyable and easy to read because they rhymed. Your books have had a great impact on my life. I learned how to read from your books. I discovered that reading can be fun and enjoyable. I now read regularly for recreation.

Your books have given me the greatest gift of all—the gift of literacy. I wanted to share this special gift with someone, so I began reading to my baby cousin, Tim, who is about five years old. When I read to him, I can see the joy in his eyes and in his laughter. I know that he felt the same way I did when I was young. Timmy can now read some of your books by himself and is beginning to realize that reading can be educational as well as fun.

I can't thank you enough for teaching me how to read. I visit the library religiously, I like reading to other people, and I just can't get enough of books.

Ernest Lam, 15

Pearl City High School, Pearl City, HI
Teacher: Mrs. Rappolt

Dear Mr. Higgan,

I have recently read your story *Jamie and Me*. I don't believe that I have related to any other story more than yours.

This past year, I started running for my school's cross-country team. To my surprise, I became their top runner and won all of my races but two. For some reason, I didn't enjoy it. I didn't despise it, but didn't enjoy it. It came to the point where I felt like I was supposed to do it, that everyone depended on me to. It didn't matter to me as much as it did to others, especially my mom. I had no choice but to run and to act like I enjoyed it.

When I read about Jamie and how she was a good runner who didn't get the same thrill out of it as her father, I was immediately comforted. To know that someone has gone through the same thing as I have in some ways made me enjoy running a little more. It's hard to see your parents love something that you're good at when you don't enjoy it yourself. They get so emotionally worked up in your races that you think to yourself, They might as well do it themselves. How are you supposed to not disappoint them?

By reading your book, my guilt over not completely fulfilling my mother's dream became a little weaker. I realized that indeed my mother is extremely proud of me and is not at all disappointed. This relieved my guilt of not enjoying running as much as I'm expected to and helped me understand all of the confusion I was feeling.

Katie Powers, 13
Strong Middle School, Middlefield, CT
Teacher: Mrs. Micowski

Dear Ms. Burnett:

As I sat on a bleak day and played my video game, I was about to win when the power went out with a zap. Devastated, I went over to my grandmother and stated one of the most common phrases known to man: "I'm bored." "Well," she said, "you could read. There is a very good book over there on the shelf called *The Secret Garden*."

As I read the back cover, I thought about what wonders might be inside and then plunged into the world of Mary Lennox. It was the sweetest, most mysterious book anyone could imagine. I bumped along with Mary across the moor. I met Martha, Weatherstaff, Dickon, and Colin. I found the key with the robin and planted flowers with Dickon. I grew with Mary, laughed, and explored. I cried when I learned that Mrs. Craven had died in the garden and shouted for joy when Colin walked. I believed in magic for the first time in my life. Thank you ever so much for a magical book that will never be forgotten.

Vanessa C. Smith, 12
Notre Dame Middle School, Pittsfield, MA
Teacher: Mrs. Belland

Dear J. R. R. Tolkien,

I have a big problem. Whenever there is something that is not meant to be touched, I want it. I don't just want it, I want it bad. So many times I daydream, thinking about having millions of dollars and what I'm going to do with them. Sometimes I dream about being the strongest stud that gets all the ladies, and sometimes I think I'm Michael Jordan, dunking over everybody. But when I'm by myself and nobody else is close to me, I fantasize about slaying dragons or being a goblin that guards its pot of treasure. There is something about fantasy that just puts me in a different world. The magic spells, the good and the bad army, and the many prophecies and hidden magical treasures just make me read more and more.

A dream that I have quite often is being able to turn invisible. What would help me to accomplish such an impossible thing? Well, a magical ring! And where would I get a magical ring when there is no such thing as magic? From fantasy, that's where. So many things I could do, if I had the ring. I could walk into a famous music group's rehearsal and enjoy the performance, or I could look into into the teacher's desk and see the exam before the test. No one would know but me.

Here is a riddle for you: "What do I have in my pocket?" I'll give you three chances, and tell you that it is not a ring. As you have probably already guessed, I have read all your books and loved them all; and as you have also probably guessed, the item that is in my pocket is a good taste for fantasy. The instant I start to read your books, I am transported into the setting. Be it a battle among many armies or exploring a cave that possesses magical treasure, I wish the book would last forever.

Shaw Wairegi, 15
Findlay High School, Findlay, OH
Teacher: Judy Withrow

Judy Blume is the author of hugely popular fiction for young people and adults. She has won many awards for her funny, honest, believable stories. She lives in New York. Another student's letter to Ms. Blume can be found in "Overcoming Difficulties."

Dear Ms. Blume,

I am writing to thank you for changing my life. I have read many of your books, if not all of them, and I realize that you offer no solution for the national debt. Likewise, you have never come forward to announce a significant medical breakthrough. Still, your candid stories detailing common events in the lives of young people have had a positive impact on my life, and I'm sure that I'm not the only young person affected by the sometimes harsh truths brought to light by them. Who's to say that the role you play in our emotional awareness isn't just as important as the national debt?

Before reading your books, I was a typical example of today's teenager, interested only in what I could seize for myself. Soon after receiving a set of your books as a gift, I became aware that I could identify with some of your characters, and could see many of my friends and classmates reflected in others. If not for your candor, it could have taken years for me to understand the effect that our actions can have on one another. It was suddenly crystal clear. Everyone is important, no matter what their imperfections, and I have come to grasp the fact that I can make a difference simply by treating everybody just as I would expect to be treated by them. This is not a new concept. It is something that I have been taught both at home and at school all of my life; but you have given me new insight into the meaning of this "golden rule" through the truth and reality of the situations about which you write.

It is hard for me to determine which book may have been most responsible for the turnaround in my thinking. There's Margaret and her anxieties, Karen and her bewilderment, Deenie and her fear—and so many more. If I must choose, however, I guess I would have to say that my very first experience affected me the most. Although I first read *Blubber* when I was in the sixth grade, I have read it at least twice a year since. It was a real eye-opener for me and never ceases to amaze me. I learned through Linda's pain, Wendy's mean streak, and Jill's ignorance—just how cruel people can and will be, given the smallest opportunity. I also learned that one is not free from responsibility simply because he is not directly involved in the situation. A conscious effort must be made to stop the pain by anyone who is aware of it. That is the only way to make a difference, and this book helped me realize that I want to make a difference.

Your works may not have moved mountains, but they have played a big part in helping me reset goals for myself. And, in a way, I have taken an important step toward the accomplishment of those goals. After all, young people hold the future of this great world in their hands, and the earlier in life that we learn to look beneath the surface of a person and into the goodness of his soul, and to treat each other with respect and dignity, the sooner we can get down to the business of solving the overpowering problems facing the world today.

This is what you have done for me through your wonderful stories about—me. Thank you again, Judy Blume.

Jayme Brod, 15
Canton High School, Canton, IL
Teacher: Mrs. Sharon Beam

Dear Ms. Cather,

I never realized how beautiful the wide-open plains and rolling hills hugging the edges of scenic highways are. Every year with great commotion, my parents would spend weeks planning out the route of our summer vacation. Our trips usually consisted of a two- or three-week scenic drive with several stops and no specific destination. To my sister and me, this ritual was a complete bore; the highlight was stopping at a gas station to buy junk food and soft drinks. It was not that we had little appreciation for the miles upon miles of neck-high weeds that whizzed past the windows of the car, but we could not seem to find the enthusiasm that our parents displayed at every single scenic and historic site at which we stopped.

A year ago, when I was a freshman, I read a book that changed the way I feel every time I gaze out of a car window. I was tired of reading science fiction and mystery, so I asked my mother if she could recommend a book for me. As she handed me the book, she warned me that it was different from what I was used to, but she knew that I would like it.

I sat down and read the first few pages of *My Antonia*. Within moments of starting, I promptly shut the book and put it back on the shelf. A few days later, during a James Bond movie marathon on television, the power went off. Reluctantly and out of sheer boredom, I dragged myself to the bookshelf and started reading *My Antonia* again. To my surprise, I could hardly put the book down. When my mother asked me if I was enjoying it, I sarcastically replied that it was just dandy. For some reason, I was afraid to let her know that I was actually committing it to memory.

By the time I finished reading the book, my mother could tell that I loved it. For weeks I would drift into a mood of reverence for everything I saw; it was all beautiful and full of meaning for me.

It was not until that summer, on our vacation, that I realized how much *My Antonia* had affected me. We had just turned off the interstate onto a scenic highway in northern Arizona. My mother's relatives had told her about a place called Pipe Spring and, of course, we were going to find it. It certainly did not look like much: an old adobe house surrounded by scrubby trees and a lot of sand at the foot of a mountain. As we proceeded along the guided tour of the area, something strange happened. Images of your vivid descriptions began to flash in my mind. Gradually, Pipe Spring began to come alive for me. I could picture the nomadic Indians of the Great Basin, camping at the spring during their yearly migrations. I could smell the rich prairie grass and hear the cowboys' shouts as they rounded up the cattle for the drive. How rich was the history of this place! It was then that I understood that I had gained respect for the history of the vast expanse of hills and plains that stretched before me, and I could hardly wait until we reached our next stop. I am so grateful that you opened my eyes.

Sarah Butcher, 16
McKinley High School, Baton Rouge, LA
Teacher: Elsie Hook

> **Anne Frank** was born on June 12, 1929, in Frankfurt on the Main, Germany. She died in March 1945 (some sources say 1944) in a concentration camp near Bergen, Germany. Anne's father found his daughter's diary after the war, when he returned to the Amsterdam warehouse where the family had hidden in an attempt to escape Nazi persecution. Another student's perspective on the book is in "War."

Dear Anne Frank,

I wish you were still alive so I could tell you how deeply your book *The Diary of a Young Girl* affected me. It not only touched my mind but also my soul. Today you would be sixty-four years old, but I visualize you more as a friend my age (thirteen years old), because we have so many things in common. We both have "dual personalities" that are similar. Also we both like to talk a lot, and some people think we are annoying at times. We both have sisters who are beautiful and perfect. Boys, movie stars, and the latest fashions are important to us, and math is not our best subject. I think you and I are very funny and like to laugh at humorous things and situations. Most important, we both love life, want to experience everything, and want to be writers.

Anne, your diary made me think about things that I never thought existed in the world. First of all, it made me think about what it is (or is not) to be free. Being Americans, we have more freedom than most people in the world. Your diary made me think about how my thirteenth year differs from yours. I have the freedom of going to a school of my choice, shop at my favorite mall, go to the movies, or go anywhere my parents think is acceptable and at any time of the day. Also, I am able to bathe, talk, walk, and go to the bathroom any time I want. Most important, I have freedom to pursue my dreams. I felt that freedom was what you missed most of all during your thirteenth year. You taught me how important that is to our existence.

Another lesson that your diary taught me was on discrimination—how terrible it is to mistreat another person because he is different. For the past four months, I have been able to think about nothing else than the way the Jews were treated by the Nazis. I don't think that I was ever discriminated against. But I now try to think before I say something negative about someone: Will that hurt them? or, Am I discriminating against them because they're different?

My parents tell me there is less prejudice in the world today than in 1942, but I know it still exists. I, like you, want to see the world as a place where people are not judged by their religion or the color of their skin, but are judged by the kindness of their heart and their contributions to mankind. I think your quotation, "In spite of everything I still believe that people are really good at heart," shouts your message to the world.

The final lesson that your book taught me is inspiration. In spite of all discrimination, humiliation, and inhumane treatment, you showed me the inner strength and courage of a young girl when things are not going well. I think of your phrase, "Chins up, stick it out, better times will come!" If you can cope with everything, so can I. Some of my classmates said, "How can Anne

Frank be an inspiration when in the end she did not fulfill her dreams."
Their statement is somewhat true, but your wish, "I want to go on living even
after my death" is inspiration to me. I realize a young author's words can live
forever.

Finally, I would like to tell you that after I read your book, I became so
fascinated with World War II and the Holocaust that I have been reading
quite a few books on the subject, such as *Anne Frank Remembered*, *The Last
Seven Months*, and *Night*. I am also excited to tell you that over my Christmas
break from school, as part of my Christmas gift, I will be going to the Holocaust Museum in Washington, D.C. There my thoughts will be focused on you
and our spirits will touch.

Natasha Gaziano, 13
St. Mary Magdalen School, Altamonte Springs, FL
Teacher: Ms. Rose Marie Williams

Alice Hoffman is the author of several books, including two bestsellers, *Turtle Moon* and *Seventh Heaven*. She lives in Boston with her husband and two young sons.

Dear Ms. Alice Hoffman,

When I was in the seventh grade, I received *At Risk* from my mom. I read it right away, and found it to be the most well-written novel I have ever read.

Growing up in a small town, I have never known anyone with AIDS or HIV. I knew the symptoms, how it could be spread, and how it could be prevented. But once I read this book, I felt like I knew more about how a person with AIDS really feels. It made me realize that a person with HIV or AIDS doesn't lie in bed all the time or spend the rest of his or her life in a hospital. In fact, I believe the opposite is true, like in the novel. Amanda has a full and active life and certainly doesn't mope around feeling sorry for herself!

I also saw how much the family and friends of someone with HIV or AIDS are affected. Amanda's family has many problems that I did not even think about until I read this, such as, if she should still go to school or live the rest of her life in her bedroom. This novel made me think a lot about what I would do if someone in my family got AIDS.

I have had some intriguing discussions with my parents about this book. One was about whether or not my parents would make me switch schools if one of my peers had AIDS. I feel the same way that Jesse did in the story. I would still be good friends with that person; she would need friends more than ever.

This book really showed me that people with AIDS or HIV are not statistics, but real people, the same as they were before they got the disease. I just want to thank you, Ms. Hoffman, for writing this novel. It taught me more about HIV and AIDS than any textbook ever could.

Lisa Kamm, 17
Decorah High School, Decorah, IA

Dear Henry David Thoreau,

The trees rustle and chime from a wind that whispers the truth. I sit back in a swivel chair that creaks when I think. Fingers that never learned how to type dash across the keyboard to answer endless musings. Dancing ideas roll one after another. My eyes catch your maxims and egotistical garble. Buried in thought, I identify with the wilderness and humanity. A page of your book, leafed and bedraggled, sits down as a young man. There is no difference between the page and the man. Let us venture in discourse.

Your pondering in the collected essays of *Walden* offers me inspiration. I have recently begun a journal, where I comment on your analogies of simple truth. I read a passage and then create, feeding from your energy. I travel with your aphoristic truths to help me explore similar inexplicable ideas in my mind. As you commented in "Economy," I am a new person who "put a little dry wood under a pot . . . and whirled round the globe with the speed of birds."

Although you no longer live on this earth, you accompany me as a friend through your masterpiece, *Walden.* Anxiously thumbing through your experience of life at a pond, I talk to you. How may that be? I cannot explain. I simply sit down and something magical and mysterious happens. I think, and you comment in black-and-white writing. I solemnly ask myself a question. You answer with joviality. My palms begin to perspire while I ponder places that I have never visited.

First, I open the book of *Walden,* setting a brick down on the ground. I read and gather inspiration, spreading mortar on the brick. Then, placing a second brick, I scribble the words of my own creative construction. Together, in discussion, we erect a wall. The master and a novice build an author, brick by brick.

Here is an excerpt from my journal of commentary on quotations from chapter one, "Economy": "The better part of the man is soon plowed into the soil for compost. Although a man may collect many treasures and fortunes, the gold is worth nothing to the Universal Soul. Will there be a value to money in the experience that follows death, whether it be reincarnation or a Utopian paradise? The buried carcass of the dead citizen returns essential compounds back to the earth. A fertilizer is more important than the abstract human idea of affluence. Social classes and self-worth exist only as a relative comparison of the man to his society."

I often find opinions of yours that closely relate to mine. I have always been an individual who recognizes my own beliefs only by talking them out. Never before have I been able to obtain my own thoughts while silently reading a book. I usually have to announce my spiritual and concrete findings to the world. So now I clear my throat and prepare to begin an oratory, and soon find that the ideas I want to say out loud are already typed into a computer in front of my face. I discover an art—writing!

As a book is a part of a library, a man is part of society. There comes a time when both man and book must leave their infrastructures. Sitting down together, they inform each other. The man departs from his social position, occupation, hobby, and so on. The book is picked up to leave a dusty shelf of criticism and common interpretation. The landscape of truth can now be painted with fresh hues of intellect. More than a hundred years ago, you escaped the confinements of society by going to Walden Pond. I also venture into the unknown, where my only constraints are created by myself.

Why is it most important that you hear of my adventure into life? You are a poet in prose and probably know that this is the true basis of an original text of literature—rudimentary and unrefined approaches to the experience of our lives.

Jacob Hall Foss Kells, 17
Flour Bluff High School, Corpus Christi, TX
Teacher: Linda Vegh

Olive Ann Burns lived in Atlanta, Georgia, and made her career as a staff writer for various periodicals such as the *Atlanta Weekly. Cold Sassy Tree* was her only novel.

Dear Mrs. Burns,

Hello there! How are you doing this fine day? I am doing quite well. I'm quite ecstatic actually! I've just finished reading *Cold Sassy Tree*, and I am totally speechless! It was wonderful! The whole time I was reading the book I was in a constant trance. I was like a little kid at Christmas! The words of the book flowed through my system and changed my outlook on life.

I live in a small town, just like Cold Sassy. Everybody knows everybody else's business. That is one fact that I do not like about my small town, but I enjoy reading about people in similar situations. It made me realize that even though I cannot prevent others' curiosity, I can respect them for it. It keeps people out of trouble and in some cases prevents some unseen tragedy from occurring, for the simple fact that the people involved do not want to be "talked about."

This book also gave me a sense of the importance of family. We moved to Ubly from Detroit when I was four, and while making that move, we left all of our relatives behind. Our closest relative lives over a hundred miles away. I think that having a grandfather like Rucker Blakeslee around all of the time would be quite an experience. Instead of having a father and a grandfather, it would be like having two fathers.

Will was the person that Rucker had the most influence on, but he also influenced the whole town. I would like to have that stature someday. A great leader. A person who could lead a city, a state, or even a country to uncharted regions. I would love to give peace, happiness, advice, and everything else I could to everyone who looked up to me. The responsibility would be a major stress factor, but I think that I could overcome that with the great feeling my services could provide. If I could do that I would be happy forever, because I made a difference.

Thank you, Olive Ann Burns for this extraordinary experience! I have never read a book of this caliber, and I probably never will again. I appreciate your work very much!

Andrew Kneffel, 18
Ubly High School, Ubly, MI
Teacher: Nancy Elliot

William H. Armstrong grew up in Lexington, Virginia, and now teaches history at the Kent School in Kent, Connecticut. He lives on a rocky hillside overlooking the Housatonic River. His other works include *Study Is Hard Work*, *The Peoples of the Ancient World*, and *My Animals*.

Dear William H. Armstrong:

When I finished reading *Sounder*, I was very upset with you because I felt depressed and my whole day was ruined. I like books with happy endings, especially when animals are involved. When the beginning of the story was sad, I somehow believed that you were saving the happy part for the end. I even thought that there would be cute little puppies that would look exactly like Sounder. How wrong I was!

My mom heard me crying and asked me what was wrong. I told her that *Sounder* was a terrible book and that I was angry at my reading teacher for putting it on my summer reading list. My mom asked me if she should read the book, too. She did, and after she finished it, we had a long talk about many things. Now I believe that your book helped me to grow up and to stop looking at the world "through rose-colored glasses." I see now that everyone's life is not as happy as mine and that I was a little bit selfish because I didn't even want to hear about the heartache of others. I found out that, unfortunately, life does not have a happy ending for everyone.

Last year in social studies, I learned all about the sharecroppers and their way of life. Now I realize that I only learned definitions and that I never really learned to feel what this life was like. Your book gave me this feeling and woke me up.

I started to think about many other things—poverty, hardship, and the sadness of other people. So many times when these kinds of stories are on the news at night, I switch them off because I don't want to know about unpleasant things. Your book did not allow me to do this—I had to face the fact that there is suffering in the world.

I always say that I want to help others, but now I know that before I can do that I have to understand what their world is like. You have taught me that books are not here just for my entertainment. There is a much more important purpose. They are here to help me to learn, to feel, and to laugh and to cry with others. I wrote you a little poem that sums up my feelings:

When at first I read your book
I was a little girl,
Whose only thought was of myself
And of my perfect world.

You made me see in many ways
That I am very blessed.

I never realized this before—
To this I must confess.

I've tried to force my mind to grow.
I think I've "seen the light."
So now I'll go into the world
To try to make it right.

Thank you for helping me to become a better person by reading your book!

Christina Martini, 12
St. Charles School, Staten Island, NY
Teacher: Mrs. Adamiszyn

Madeleine L'Engle is the author of many popular and acclaimed books for children and adults. Her works include novels, essays, plays, and poetry. She is perhaps best known for *A Wrinkle in Time*, which won a Newbery Medal. Other works include *Camilla*, the Austin Family series, the Cannon Tallis Mystery series, and *The Other Side of the Sun*. She lives and works in New York City.

Dear Ms. L'Engle,

You don't know this yet, but you're a good friend of mine. I suppose that sounds pretty funny coming from a thirteen-year-old girl you've never met, but it's true. Your books, especially *A Wind in the Door*, have meant a lot to me.

When I read *A Wind in the Door*, I realized that it's not stupid or childish to dream about fanciful, science-fiction-like people (or should I say beings), places, and events. After all, we know very little about what's outside our solar system, and today's fantasy may be tomorrow's fact.

I could never put into words the feelings you described as having no need for words—not thinking, but just being. *Being* is a word that confuses some people. I can't explain it; I can only understand it. I never knew there were others who thought thoughts like mine until I read your book. I found out I wasn't alone, and that's a good feeling.

I always figured there was an explanation for everything, but after I read your book I realized that some things we cannot understand, but only accept. Well, I guess some scientists might disagree, but you and I know the truth. The deep insight you use in your book is like nothing I've seen before. It really made me think.

From your books I can tell that you believe in God and His ways the same way I do. I thought it was wonderful when you said He makes sure each star has a name so they won't feel unwanted. You, like me, think of Him as the source of goodness.

When love was described in your words, you opened up a whole new world in my mind. How misunderstood love is in the "real world." The more you have, the more you can give away. You have to know who you are to know others. This philosophy is simple, but true. If only everyone could believe this, the world would be such a better place.

In your book, size and distance are irrelevant, and everyone is equal. With this book I can escape into the world you've created and get away from my own problems. It's a haven no one can destroy. Thank you for all you've done, Ms. L'Engle.

Breeann Songer, 13
Ellicottville Central, Ellicottville, NY
Teacher: Mary Terry

Carol Ryrie Brink was born in Idaho in 1895 and made her home in La Jolla, California. She wrote books for both children and adults. Her works include *Anything Can Happen on the River, Four Girls on a Homestead*, and *Buffalo Coat*. She also contributed short stories and poems to various periodicals.

Dear Carol Brink,

Glancing over my bookshelf, my eyes meet upon many books that I have come to love as I grow up: *Where the Red Fern Grows; The Lion, the Witch and the Wardrobe; Charlie and the Chocolate Factory;* and *Mary Poppins.* Finally, my eyes light on *Caddie Woodlawn.* It's hard for me to put my finger on exactly what I like about it. My first thoughts are that Caddie is the kind of girl I'd want to be. It's hard to imagine my conservative little self as a wild tomboy who runs around on the prairie and befriends Indians. Now, I have no problem with Indians; I think they're a beautiful people, but one look at a tomahawk and a scalp belt and I'd pass out cold.

I have to confess that sometimes during class, I'm off in space. Actually, I'm not in space, but on the prairie. I think about Caddie and what makes her so special, so important that a book was written about her. Even her name is unique. Everything she said was what she really felt. I've always been afraid to say exactly what I feel. Caddie respected people and they, in turn, respected her back. Maybe that's one way I can be like her.

I thrive on learning. While most kids enjoy plopping down in front of the TV and becoming zombies, I'd prefer to sit by a fire and read the whole day long. Did that surprise you? Do you ever wonder what's wrong with kids these days? Hey, we're not so bad. If you gave us an inch, we wouldn't take a mile. We'd say, "Thank you." I don't believe in generation gaps. In my mind, there's no such thing. My definition for generation gap is a stubborn person, one who's not willing to become more open-minded. I love to learn something about the past and I'm sure that some adults would be willing to change their ways.

One of the reasons I love *Caddie Woodlawn* is because of the time period. There are so many things that history books don't tell you. They don't tell you how the people felt, what they were going through, and they usually try to stay neutral. (No offense to you history book writers.) Many people think that if you've read a history book, you know it all. WRONG! This period of time fascinates me so much that I can never read enough about it. The people in this time knew what was really important: family, which is the one thing I hold dearest.

I'd love to be like Caddie, to explore the adventures of life during that time and to live in history forever. But for now, I'll stay myself and be what I am, because that's what Caddie would have done.

Jennifer Spearie, 13
St. Aloysius School, Springfield, IL
Teacher: Roberta Hull

Letters about two of **John Steinbeck**'s other novels, *The Pearl* and *Of Mice and Men*, can be found in "Overcoming Difficulties" and "The Power of Conviction."

Dear Mr. Steinbeck,

Last summer when I read your book *The Grapes of Wrath*, I had to take breaks every few chapters because the story was so powerful. I had to stop to let myself think about what your story was saying. The Joad family's struggles during the Depression were teaching me many lessons about people's reactions to extreme hardship and how all people are connected.

Seeing the harsh reality of poverty moved me deeply. As the family's living and psychological conditions worsened, I first felt sorrow, then an enormous helplessness. It seemed like everything was completely out of control, yet the Joads continued on. They seemed to grow even stronger. By the end of the book, I felt drained and had many questions about what had happened to the Joads.

As I thought about my questions, I could see your message was that taking responsibility is a way to accomplish anything. I could see that communities working together can be a way out of poverty and desperation. I especially liked the message Jim Casy preached about how each person is a little part of the universe and how we all need to find each other and pull together.

You have shown not only the misery in the world, but also the goodness and generosity that can emerge from darkness. The most poignant example of this was at the end. The setting was the most desolate, and the Joads' fate seemed the dreariest of the entire story. Amid a torrent of troubles, driving rain, and mud, the family sought shelter. In an old barn, they found two other frightened, starving travelers. Rosasharon had just lost her last hope, her newborn baby. But then she gave the only thing she had left, her milk, to one of the travelers to give him a last chance at hope. I could see that however desperate or impoverished the situation, people can still be heroic and kind.

What I learned about myself from this book was that I probably have an inner reservoir of strength, courage, and persistence to call upon in times of seeming hopelessness. I also learned from my sadness for the Joads that I have strong empathy for people in misery. And I began to see how far I can reach.

Your book has shown me the despair of poverty, but it has also taught me to take responsibility and to see how much we need each other. One way I can do this is to become a writer. Writers show people what they are doing and who they really are. Unless we can see what we are doing wrong, we can't solve our problems. My writing could show people that there can still be hope when they give of themselves to one another. Your book has helped me find my place.

Elisabeth Wurtmann, 14
Valley Middle School, Burnsville, MN
Teacher: Tom Kelly

Dear Elisabeth Peters,

I would like to congratulate you on one of the best books I have ever read. Because you have written so many books, all of them good, let me clarify. I am talking about your first book in the Amelia Peabody series, *The Crocodile on the Sandbank.*

But I am getting ahead of myself. My name is Sarah Thompson and I am thirteen years old. I started reading your books when I was twelve. My mother picked up four of your books at the storekeeper's suggestion, due to my lack of reading material. To be perfectly honest, at first I thought your books sounded too romantic for my taste. But lo and behold, I found that they were perfectly clean and well written.

Anyway, I wanted to tell you how Amelia, Emerson, and eventually Ramses helped me discover a very important part of myself that I didn't know about. I discovered that I had neglected my rights as a woman. Guys at school are always assuming that girls are stupid or, if they are smart, they are considered nerds. In fact, even some male teachers also act sexist. An example is a teacher of mine (who will remain nameless) who, when he was passing out tests, came to a girl who got an A. When he handed her the test, he pointedly said, "Pretty good for a girl." That threw me (not to mention her) into a rage.

But through your literature, I've sought refuge from this sexist world. Emerson was the perfect man, but my favorite character is Amelia. She stood up for herself and wasn't afraid to voice her opinion. She become a role model of mine. My mother reads your books, too, and she says I remind her of Ramses, but I don't see the resemblance.

But you killed my favorite villain! I wish you hadn't killed Sethos. Now Emerson doesn't have anyone to be jealous of or to fight. I suppose however, it had to happen sometime, but had I been the writer, I would have given Emerson that privilege.

At any rate, I am out of things to say, other than that I love your work, so please keep it up. P.S. What is your favorite book that you have written yourself? That any other person has written?

Sarah Thompson, 14
Lakeshore Junior High School, Stevensville, MI
Teacher: Mrs. Carol Campbell

war

Jerzy Kosinski (1933-1991) taught English at Wesleyan, Princeton, and Yale Universities and wrote several novels. *The Painted Bird* was based on his childhood in Europe during World War II. He won the National Book Award for *Steps*. He was an avid polo player, skier, and photographer.

Dear Mr. Jerzy Kosinski,

This weekend, I finished reading your story *The Painted Bird* and I haven't been able to leave it behind. In the past, stories about the Holocaust have seemed very unreal and distant to me. When reading such books, it is easy to make yourself forget that the fictional story you are reading is rooted in truth. Countless shocking pictures of skeletal survivors and gigantic heaps of clothing stripped from bodies before cremation had long since dimmed my anguish and sense of outrage at the needless suffering of millions during Hitler's reign. It was your moving story of a young boy, fighting for survival on his own, that helped me break down the barriers I had build up. It was impossible to remain detached from your story. Because I was so enthralled by it, I was forced to come to terms with my own horror, guilt, and sadness surrounding the Holocaust.

The Painted Bird was so powerful because of its skillful blending of the real and unreal. In the back of your mind, you know that people like the cold SS officers and brutal German peasants existed and that the horrible, nightmarish things described in the story were not that uncommon. However, since I have never had to fight for my life or been faced with the same situations as the boy, to me it seemed as though this story could exist only in my nightmares. But in the back of my mind, I knew that such things really happened, and no matter how hard I tried to ignore it, that fact would never go away.

I kept thinking about how much the boy had been influenced by the violent acts he had witnessed. His whole view of the world changed and, as a result, he became an entirely different person by embracing Communism, rejecting his parents, putting faith in the superstitious views of the peasants, and reveling in violence. Had he not accepted violence, he probably would have died several times over. Would it have been a "better" fate for someone to remain true to his or her childhood ideals and be killed, or to do whatever was necessary to survive? Everyone had to make this same choice during the Holocaust, whether Jew, peasant, or Nazi, but I can only struggle to answer this question for myself.

Later on, I began thinking about my own family roots in Germany. I am only the third generation on my father's side to be born in America. Suddenly, the boy and the peasants weren't as far removed from me as I would like them to be. In fact, some (or many) of my own ancestors may have gone through similar experiences. The protective, dreamy sheen of the book allowed me to ignore that fact while taking in the story, but afterward it was impossible for me to ignore. The boy is never named in the story, because he represents everyone who experienced suffering and changed because of it during World War II. He could be anyone, even someone in my own family.

Today, it seems very unlikely that violence could spread on such a wide scale as it did during the Holocaust. However, in your story, violence always lurked under the surface of the most peaceful setting. Under the right set of circumstances, anyone, even the boy himself, could lash out. Even more frightening, no one seemed to have a sense of what was right and wrong. To them (and even their victims on occasion), their savage actions seemed perfectly justified.

This book made me realize how far removed I am from the times and experiences of my own ancestors. It would be impossible for me to judge the actions of anyone in the past, since I have little knowledge of the pressures they faced and the ethical system they operated under. I can, however, examine the results of their actions and learn from their experiences. If we are to avoid future worldwide disasters like the Holocaust, we must all bond together. In *The Painted Bird*, suspicions were raised and violence erupted when differences separated two parties. Today, racially motivated crimes remind us that such problems still exist. To live together in peace, we must not forget but respect each other's differences. By building on the past, we can make the future positive for everyone.

Jamie L. Pflasterer, 18
Illinois Mathematics & Science Academy, Aurora, IL
Teacher: Dr. L. Chott

Dear Anne Frank,

I have never met you, nor you me, but I feel as if I know you intimately. I read your diary—I hope you don't mind. Since your death, it has been printed and reprinted, and people from everywhere have read and loved it. I just finished reading your last entry—to Kitty. I am Jewish like you, but I live a happily normal life. I am not at all without friends my own age and otherwise. I live in a big old farmhouse, and I am free to come and go as I please. But still I can see many mirrors between our lives. Maybe as Pim said, these are just stages that every girl goes through, for sometimes—not half as often as you did—but sometimes I find myself feeling frustrated, babied, and misunderstood, just like you did. When that happens to me, I grouch around, argue, and reply rudely when people talk to me. I didn't realize that I wasn't alone in feeling like that until I read your diary.

I read your diary in the first place because I've always been interested in what it was like to be Jewish during the Holocaust. I've tried to read every book on the subject that I can get my hands on. I thought it would be another book about a girl in hiding. I didn't realize it would be so different. Your diary is unique because it's not about the war, but about what happens because of the war. You talk about daily life, about your troubles and annoyances, about food, people, hopes, dreams—everything that was an issue for you. Also, you wrote as these things were happening, not fifty years later. And your diary was better than books by people who got their information as I did, by reading, for everything that you wrote about really happened to you—you aren't just writing about something you heard about.

A while ago, I went to a Holocaust seminar for junior-high students, and heard a man talk about his experiences in a concentration camp during World War II. That made an impression on me, too. You know, Anne, your two experiences are infinitely different, and yet infinitely similar. You both experienced being cut off from the world, and you both waited for the war and your oppression to end. But he lived. You died. He spent the war traveling from concentration camp to concentration camp. You spent most of the war in the Secret Annex. Put your two experiences together, and you get the Holocaust.

One instance where you especially affected me was when you wrote that letter to Pim, about how you didn't need a mother anymore. When I read that, I realized how sometimes I too fool and pity myself so that I will appear big in my mind. I now try to do better, and not think: Alas, I am alone against an unyielding world. Ah, such a sad lot is mine! So Pim has taken *me* down from *my* pedestal, too.

You've inspired me, Anne, to start keeping a diary. So far, I've written just four entries, but then I've been keeping it for only four days. Actually,

I've always kept a diary, but those diaries are not me, but rather nice little books full of nice little details about my nice little life. But this diary really *is* me, not what I would like others to think of me. Diaries are wonderful things. I know you'll agree.

I'm not the only one you've inspired. I have also read a diary by a girl named Zlata Filipovic *[Zlata's Diary]*. She too started a diary after reading yours. Like you, she lived in a time of war, and though she was not forced into hiding, she could hardly step outside for fear of being shot. She is still alive, and her diary has been printed and read by many. But then, I can relate far, far more to you than to her—not because of your different situations, or that you are Jewish and she's not, but because of the way you described your emotions, and how closely they match my own.

After reading your diary, I feel that I can view not only the world, but also myself with greater understanding. Also, I now have a diary that will always be there for me to confide in when I need it most. And I've gained a greater compassion for and interest in the affairs of countries such as Bosnia, because you've made me realize that the tragedies we hear about in a reporter's quick, even voice on the seven o'clock news happen to real people like myself, not just to numbers or names. I can honestly say that reading your diary has made an impression on me that will last for the rest of my life.

Molly E. Richman, 11
Pennsylvania Homeschoolers, Kittanning, PA
Teacher: Susan P. Richman

Phung Thi Le Ly Hayslip was born in a small village near Danang in central Vietnam. She married an American GI and came to the United States near the end of the Vietnam War. She now lives in southern California with her three sons. Her life story was the basis for *Heaven and Earth,* the third film in Oliver Stone's Vietnam trilogy. She is the founder of the East Meets West Foundation, a charitable relief and world peace organization.

Dear Phung Thi Le Ly Hayslip,

I am a twelve-year-old Vietnamese girl, the first generation of my family to be born in the United States. My mother grew up in Saigon, and my father grew up just outside of Saigon in the countryside. My parents came here in the mid-1970s.

I have recently finished reading your autobiography, *When Heaven and Earth Change Places.* When I was reading it, I finally began to "see" my parents' side of the war. I had no idea they had to live through all that turmoil. Your story helped me learn how sacrifices are one of the most important things about war.

My parents have never discussed much about the war. They have told me how they finally managed to get on a plane and travel here, but they've never mentioned anything about their hardships during the war. I think it is because it was too painful for them to relive what they had gone through and struggled to forget. Some relatives from my father's side died during the time, but none of my mom's. My mother's relatives thought she was missing for a couple of years though. They even thought that she had died. After finishing your life story, I realize how important my family really is to me. Despite growing up in America, I still uphold old Vietnamese traditions.

Many of your readers will be dumbfounded after reading about your struggle. Many may even say that the events that occurred could not have possibly happened, even though they did. After exposing that much displeasure about the Vietnam War, readers will see your life from a victim's point of view, not an observer's.

Your life story does not make me view the world as a horrid place, but a place where anything can happen. A place where misunderstanding and [violence] are no joke. It also makes me see the world as a place where happiness can be lurking around the corner, awaiting you in your darkest hour. You just need to look in the right place to find what you really want.

People no longer criticize me for what I am and look like, because I am proud to stand up for who I am and what I represent. I am glad to have a richly cultured heritage, because it teaches me about myself. I never could stand people prejudging me and discriminating against me because I was not like them. I have learned to ignore and keep away from [people like that].

Julia Le (Le Nam Giao-Julia), 13
Wilbraham High School, Wilbraham, MA
Teacher: Mrs. Stacy Dwyer

Jane Yolen has published more than a hundred books for children and adults, including *Sky Dogs, Children of the Wolf, Tam Lin,* and *Dove Isabeau.* Along with her picture books and short stories, she has published numerous novels. She lives in western Massachusetts.

Dear Jane Yolen,

Whenever I am tempted to complain about some relatively minute detail of my life—too much homework, too many violin exercises, too many brussels sprouts—I think of Gemma [in *Briar Rose*] and remember how safe and free my life is. A grouchy teacher, a stuck backpack zipper, an abysmal score on a math quiz, a misplaced retainer, a jammed locker—all seem silly and minuscule when compared to Gemma's traumas and all the horrors of the Holocaust.

Although I have been interested in learning more about the Holocaust for several years, I never fully understood what it might have *felt* like to be trapped unfairly in such a terrifying situation until I read *Briar Rose. Number the Stars* and *The Diary of a Young Girl* are both gripping and emotional stories, but neither one seems as immediate or as real as your book. From the very beginning of *Briar Rose,* I could sympathize entirely with Becca's feelings as she tries to understand Gemma's past. Although Becca is not an only child (I am), Shana and Sylvia exclude her so completely that she feels like one. I understand Becca's solitariness and her contentment to live her own life independently and happily. I admire her endurance and her spunkiness.

The Holocaust took place fifty years ago. That, by Gemma's calculations, is half of forever. To me (I'm thirteen), the 1940s might as well be the 1740s. It was a long time ago. Because *Briar Rose* takes place in the present, a period I can appreciate, I was able to bring myself closer to the events that changed Gemma's life and created a mystery that Becca has to solve. If such terrible things happened to Becca's grandmother, the same terrible things might have happened to my own relatives, to grandparents and great aunts and uncles, to people I know and love. What happened at Auschwitz and Chelmno is still present in our world today as long as there are Gemmas here to remind us or Beccas to root out the truth.

Gemma came to my mind last summer, when I had the opportunity to visit Terezin, the infamous children's concentration camp near Prague. When my parents first asked me whether or not I wanted to go with them, my reaction was to say yes *and* no. I was curious, but I was afraid.

Thank you for writing *Briar Rose*. If your book has touched others as much as it has touched me, we can be sure that there will never be another holocaust.

Elizabeth Archibald, 13
East Granby Middle School, East Granby, CT
Teacher: Mrs. Poskus

Dear Zlata Filipovic,

Your book *Zlata's Diary,* made me think about war. At first, I thought wars could not affect a simple girl in San Francisco. When I read your book, I discovered that they could happen in your own backyard and they affect everyone. What if I had heard bombings day and night in my own neighborhood? I probably would have begged my mother and father to let our family move to a different country. When I read that your friend, Nina, died in a neighborhood park, it made me think about what I would feel like if my friend had been playing in a playground and she was killed. I would have been angry and sad—How could these people kill a sweet, innocent girl?

After I read your book, I started to get more involved in current events. I heard and read about the horrifying wars that were taking place all over the world. I saw people's houses ruined, neighborhoods looking awful, cherished memories disappearing, and the young and old dead. I felt terrible that these wars were probably going on all my life and I was not paying much attention to them. I hear about these appalling things and just pray and yearn that things will become better for the people who have to live through them.

People's lives are ruined and families separated all over the world because of wars. Hundreds and thousands of people are getting killed over an argument about who owns a piece of land. I think that it is really meaningless to start a war over this problem.

I hope that in the future we will have peace, and no one will ever have to go through what you or anybody else has because of war. I wish that we could live together as one, instead of being split because of race, sex, religion, where we live, culture, and many other things that keep us away from reaching the goal [of unity].

Shilpa Ramaiya, 12
St. Gabriel School, San Francisco, CA
Teacher: Ms. Lynn Grier

Bette Green was born in a small town in Arkansas, and later lived in Memphis, Tennessee, and Paris. She now lives in Brookline, Massachusetts, with her husband. She is celebrated for the strong emotional response that readers have to her books. Her other novels include *Philip Hall Likes Me, I Reckon Maybe; Them That Glitter and Them That Don't;* and *Morning Is a Long Time Coming,* the companion volume to *The Summer of My German Soldier.*

Dear Bette Green,

I finished *The Summer of My German Soldier* the other night and I just wanted to tell you that it was an excellent book. It was so well written that I was crying at the end. This book gave me such a different perspective on how prejudiced our country is. I hope I'm not prejudiced like some of the people in your book. I try to be fair, but it is so easy when choosing between people to choose the one most like me.

I also really began to see how lucky I am to be part of a family that accepts me for who I am, and not to be abused like Patty was in your book. A deep feeling of helplessness swept over me as I was reading parts of your book about her father's abuse. I guess I would have run out to try to help, like Antone did too. Were you beaten as a child? Don't think of me as rude or anything, but you described Patty's feelings about her abusive father so well that I almost felt you were trying to get out some of your own hidden feelings.

Your book has changed the way I think about a lot of things. One example of this is my feelings about World War II. I always thought that the Axis powers were so awful, because they captured our soldiers, as well as Jews, and put them in concentration camps. But Americans put all of the Japanese into camps like the Germans did. We did not force them to work to death or murder them, but we did take American citizens (as they were at that time), and gathered them into certain areas. I can't even begin to think how mad they were at other Americans.

Another way the book has affected me is in my feelings toward others. Since reading it, I have tried to be more accepting of others, their beliefs and their cultures. As you can see, I really enjoyed your book and I think it has changed my life. I am anxious to read the sequel.

Linetta Alley, 14
Turner Ashby High School, Bridgewater, VA
Teacher: Mrs. Sellers

Sook Nyul Choi was born in Pyongyang, North Korea, and came to the United States to attend Manhattanville College. She taught school in New York City for almost twenty years while raising her two daughters. She now lives in Cambridge, Massachusetts, and has made a career out of writing and teaching creative writing to high-school students. Her other works include *Echoes of the White Giraffe* and *Halmoni and the Picnic*.

Dear Sook Nyul Choi,

A couple of weeks ago, I was in a play called *I Never Saw Another Butterfly,* which touched me more than anything else; that is, anything before I read your book. I was searching for a book in my brother's book collection when I saw your book, *Year of Impossible Goodbyes* [about the Korean War]. I wasn't really looking for an interesting book, just one to satisfy a class requirement. I didn't know that after I read your book it would have such an effect on my feelings about life and death.

The book was by far the best book I had ever read. I cried and laughed at the same moments. I actually felt I was right there, feeling everything that Sookan was feeling.

It made me ask many questions. One of them was, "Why do people have to be so harsh and cruel?" Can't they just settle with what they have and be happy with it, instead of taking everything for granted? I looked deep inside myself and my heart to find the best answer possible. The answer I was able to come up with was that people today are too jealous and selfish to be happy with life. They see something that someone else has and they want it. They don't care who they have to hurt or even kill, just as long as they get whatever they want. I never knew why people liked to fight in wars and gangs. This reason helped me realize just why they do it.

Your book also made me ask myself why countries couldn't just leave Korea alone. It seemed to be a strong, glorious, wealthy nation until the Japanese and Communist Russians came in, took their property, pride, and values, and tried to rule their lives.

The last question that I asked myself was, "Why didn't the Koreans fight back?" Why didn't they join together and force the other countries out of their land? I do not know the answers to all of these questions, but I do know that the Koreans were extremely unhappy.

Year of Impossible Goodbyes was a wonderfully written book. To me, a point was made—War is harsh and uncontrollable. If everyone read this book, then maybe they would think more about not hurting people and more about people's feelings and their personal point of views on life.

You have inspired me into thinking about maybe writing my own book someday. I would dedicate it: "To the author of *Year of Impossible Goodbyes*, my inspiration. May God bless you and grant you your most precious wishes throughout your life."

Lisa Snyder, 14
William Henry Harrison Junior High School, Harrison, OH
Teacher: Ms. Rice

Eliezer (Elie) Wiesel was born in Sighet, Romania, in 1928 and came to the United States in 1956. He has worked as a foreign correspondent, writer, lecturer, and professor of Judaic studies, philosophy, and religious studies. His works include *Dawn, The Town Beyond the Wall*, and *One Generation After.*

Dear Elie,

I must honestly say that I did not enjoy your tragic novel *Night*, but then I doubt that you wrote it to be enjoyed. I was assigned to read *Night* and literally groaned when I discovered it was about the Holocaust. I felt I had heard enough about this horrible time period and didn't understand why teachers persisted in making us read such graphic accounts. I thought I realized the terror and didn't want to hear one more awful story. Throughout the entire novel, my stomach was tight and my eyes watered. At times I had to set the book down and walk away to relieve my mind and heart of the agony I was constantly feeling for Elle. I hated every page and every word that was a continual reminder of the depravity of man.

I tried to relate with what Elle was going through, but obviously I could not. There was no common ground whatsoever. *Night* forced me to realize there was no way I could every truly comprehend the horror. I believe it was this that made me even more frustrated with the novel. After all the years I had been taught about the Holocaust and all the stories I had read, nothing compared to yours. Never had I read such a powerful account in my life. *Night* assaulted me with the graphic details others were afraid to tell, and it was this that opened my eyes.

As I finished the book, I threw it across my room, angered and disgusted. I recall looking at it lying on the floor and never wanting to think about its contents again. I froze, and cringed as the realization of my thought sunk in. The reason I hated the book, the reason I didn't want to read the book in the first place, was that I didn't want to think about it. I convinced myself I already knew everything. I told myself I didn't need to hear any more. I tried as hard as I could to protect myself from the full terror of the truth. But I hated myself and the way I was hiding. My actions were as ignorant as those of the average passive citizen during the Holocaust. Like them, I didn't want to know everything, but your emotional and frighteningly true novel forced me to see.

Looking back, I'm glad I read *Night*. Not only did it make me aware of the wall of ignorance I was trying to build around myself, but it helped me to take that wall down. I will never look forward to reading such heart-wrenching novels as yours, but I will do it if only to educate myself. Thank you for the courage you had to write *Night*. Never again will I shut myself off from reality. I will try my hardest to face it and learn from the truth.

Emily Judge, 15
Wheaton-Warrenville South High School, Wheaton, IL
Teacher: Mrs. McKenna

life-long
inspiration

To Mr. Shel Silverstein:

~~*Dear Mr. Silverstein,*~~

How about . . . Dear Shel, (?)

Hi! Guess what . . . I'm a dreamer, a wisher, a liar, a hope-er, a pray-er, a magic bean buyer, and a pretender, and—well—thanks for the invitation! It came a long time ago. I don't even remember when, but it was some Christmas. My brothers and I tore open the wrapping paper and met those two little kids peering over the edge of the world. It was us! I was the girl, Paul was the boy, and I guess David could have been the dog.

Today I took *Where the Sidewalk Ends* off the shelf again. The white cover doesn't stay on too well anymore, and it's really not that white now either. I'm still the girl; I'm seventeen. Paul's still the boy; he's fifteen. David's thirteen and, yes, he's probably still the dog. We're still past the EDGE KEEP OFF! sign. For that, I thank you!

Do you know that you have been everywhere with us? That Christmas we took our brand-new book to all of the family visiting places. We read the poems to our little cousins. When the adults were busy doing adult things, we read the poems to ourselves. At night Mom or Dad read them to us. (Sometimes they still do.) You came with us on long car trips. We sat by your fire and your flax-golden tales when the rain put the campfire out.

You know what else? We've been everywhere with you. We've built the treehouse, the free house, the secret you and me house. We did the home-made boat. We've been acrobats. We've had gashes and rashes and purple bumps. And I just know that you used the poem "Sarah Cynthia Silvia Stout would not take the garbage out" only because you hadn't yet thought of "Andrea Christine Veronica Urb would not take it to the curb."

Next year I'm going to college. Guess who's coming with me . . .

I'll try to remember the forgotten language. I promise. And I'll enter this abandoned house once more. And I'll be king if the world was crazy because, you know, your nonsense still makes sense now. I find more wisdom and more life in a poem written on the neck of a running giraffe than in many of my long-winded textbooks.

So, Mr. Shel Silverstein, thank you! Thank you! Thank you! Thank you! I'll remember you when I'm listening to the mustn'ts. And don't worry—you're not off the hook yet.

Andrea Urbiel, 17
Divine Child High School, Detroit, MI
Teacher: Mrs. Marcia Closson

index

About The Center for the Book

The Center for the Book in the Library of Congress was created in 1977 to stimulate public interest in books and reading. Through its reading promotion network of 29 affiliated state centers and more than 120 national civic and educational organizations, it reaches into every community with promotion themes, television and radio messages, exhibits, and essay contests such as *Letters About Literature*. The center is small, catalytic, and a successful public-private partnership—for it relies on contributions to support its projects and publications. We are grateful to *Read* magazine for its cosponsorship of the *Letters About Literature* contest and to Weekly Reader and Conari Press for donating part of the proceeds from *Dear Author* to the state centers for the book.

–John Y. Cole, Director
Center for the Book

Letters About Literature

For further information about how to enter the "Letters About Literature" contest, call *Read* magazine at 203-638-2400.

Teacher's Guide Available

Conari Press now offers an easy-to-use, inspirational teacher's guide to *Dear Author* written by educators. It includes guidelines and suggestions on how to teach a *Dear Author* lesson in your classroom as well as a list of creative activities.

For more information on obtaining a copy, contact your local bookstore, or write to:

Dear Author Teacher's Guide
Conari Press
2550 Ninth Street, Suite 101
Berkeley, CA 94710